STAR KNIGHT SAGA
SAGA
Book 1: REAVERS OF THE VOID

by Bradford C. Walker

DEDICATION

This book, and series, is dedicated to the memory of my great uncle Kenneth Holm and to the memory of the battleship he served upon when he died: U.S.S. *Oklahoma.*

May you and your shipmates rest forever in peace. The glories of fiction pale in comparison to the desperate heroics you and your mates did at Pearl Harbor, but they will keep alive your memory long after it would otherwise fade.

ACKNOWLEDGMENTS

This book would not exist if not for the support of my backers on Indiegogo. There were 96 in all, and most of them preferred to remain anonymous. Some did not, and they will be acknowledged by name: Iris C. Paustian, Edward Toon, and Justin Williams. I am grateful to all of you for putting your money behind this project, and I hope that you like what you got.

Cover courtesy of ArtAnon.

1 ARRIVAL

It is the year of our Lord 3001. On the fifth of January a *Longboat*-class cutter, *Baden-Powell*, emerged from hyperspace. Shaped like a leaf, with a single tri-barreled turret on its dorsal hull, its golden hull glimmered in the reflected light from the system's sun.

The cutter's master--Sir Ramsey Hennepin of the Vatican Solar Guard, Lord of the Seat of Roland--entered the ship's bridge. He cut a striking, charismatic, and clean-cut figure as one expects of an elite fighting man. Sir Ramsey's sergeant-at-arms sat in the co-pilot's seat, Sibley Hall. Hall was an older warrior, barrel-chested and bearing a white beard.

"We've arrived at New Edinburgh, my lord" Sibley said.

"Right on schedule, Sibley," Ramsey said as he took the pilot's chair, "We should get our welcome presently."

The ship's main viewscreen flashed a warning of an incoming transmission. Sibley answered it. An approaching cruiser belonging to the ruling House Ireton appeared on screen. Its hammerhead-like profile indicated it to be one of the *Ferguson* class. Then the screen changed to show her captain's face.

"Lord Roland, I presume?" the Captain said.

"I am", Ramsey said, "This is my man Sibley. Your duke expects us."

The Captain nodded. "I am Sir Harold Harrison, Captain of the *MacCullough*. Welcome to New Edinburgh, my lord. His Grace the duke dispatched us to meet you. We shall escort you to orbit."

"I appreciate the courtesy, Captain. Lead the way."

"Please form up on our wing to starboard, my lord. We shall get you through orbital traffic with all due speed."

"Understood Captain. Over and out."

The feed cut out and the viewscreen returned to the view of the *MacCullough*. Ramsey took the conn and smoothly guided Baden-Powell as requested, flying just to *MacCullough*'s starboard side. As the ships flew towards the planet, the orbital infrastructure became clear.

Massive cylindrical colonies in the ancient O'Neill style ringed the planet at its Lagrange points. The traffic of vessels and mecha between them between flowed in orderly lines coordinated by an army of traffic controllers. Ground-to-orbit traffic flew into and out of the planet's Earth-normal atmosphere in the same manner.

Sibley's son Creton rushed on to the bridge, changing the mood. He was a boy aged 10, with a traditional bowl-cut to his dark hair, wearing Ramsey's livery.

"Is that it, Father?" Creton said, pointing to the planet on the viewscreen.

"That it is, son", Sibley said with a smile. "New Edinburgh, the seat of House Ireton and capital of the Dire March."

"Do you really think Red Eyes will attack here?"

Ramsey reached over and tousled the boy's hair. "I hope not," he said, "but if what we got from Garmil's Gate is correct, then we'd be derelict in our duty to not warn the Duke in person and render what aide we may."

As the vessels passed by the nearby cluster of orbital stations, *MacCullough* hailed Baden-Powell again. "You're clear to land directly at the military spaceport, my lord. Farewell!"

"Farewell, Captain." Ramsey said, and the Solar Guard cutter turned to descend into the cloudscape of New Edinburgh.

* * *

On the outer edge of the New Edinburgh system a battleship emerged from hyperspace. It was long and thin, painted grey from stem to stern, with three tri-barreled turrets on its dorsal hull. Two were between the bow and amidships and the third mounted aft.

Emblazoned across the dorsal hull was the insignia of the Red Eyes Pirates: a red-eyed skull. From the stern, out of a ventral ramp, a dozen smaller units emerged. These units were ovoid-shaped battle pods with chicken-like legs attached, their red mono-eyes and pair of cannons combining to create a mockery of a face. Their legs swung back as the thrusters kicked in, and they surged forward ahead of the battleship.

A thin and fit young man with shoulder-length blond hair wearing a long coat with the Red Eyes insignia on the breast stepped off a lift and onto the pirate ship's bridge. He paused for a moment to make his presence known.

Another man, a giant of a man with naturally red eyes and blue skin, half again the thin man's height, turned to the crew and bellowed "Captain on the bridge!"

"As you were." The thin man walked over to the captain's chair and seated himself, "Comms, call home."

The Communications Officer, a mousy disfigured man wearing red goggles, nodded. "Aye, Captain," he said as he punched some buttons. "You're through to Hell's Heart now, sir."

On the main viewscreen a blue-skinned, red-eyed face with canine teeth, and a flowing mane of blood-red hair turned to face the Captain. "Ah, there you are, Jack. *Revenge* has arrived undetected?"

"It has, High Admiral", Jack said.

"Proceed to the forward base. Rendezvous there with the courier and proceed as planned."

"Aye, sir."

"I look forward to you bringing me that treasure, Jack. I need that haul intact and unspoiled."

"I haven't disappointed you yet, sir."

Red Eyes' smug smirk turned to a snarl. "Then don't make this the first time. I'm not done with you yet."

"Understood, sir. You'll have the jewel you desire."

"Good. I'd hate to have to make an example of you. Be ready when my sister arrives. Over and out."

The feed cut, and the viewscreen showed an asteroid field fast approaching.

"Dara's Folly," Jack said. "I'm surprised Ireton hasn't demolished this place yet."

The blue-skinned giant stepped forward to stand next to his captain. "Ireton's attention has been elsewhere for some time, Captain."

"Yes, Gori, it has, and not just because Red Eyes distracted him somehow. Let's hope Ireton's inattention persists long enough to execute this heist and get away with our prize."

On a screen attached to the captain's chair Jack brought up a picture of a young woman. She had bold green eyes and bright fire-red hair, wore a full-length green dress with gold trim. She was of prime marrying age, about twenty years, and had a smile that could warm a room during a cold winter night.

"Some jewel", Gori said. "This is what the Admiral wants, eh?"

"Yes, the Songbird of Second Salisbury, and the sole daughter of its master, Count Robin—Gabriela."

Gori gave a cock-eyed look to his captain. "Countess Gabriela Robin? She's the prize?"

"Indeed."

"A lot of men are going to die for this, aren't they?"

Jack let out a laugh that filled the bridge of *Redalen's Revenge*. "Gori, your gift for understatement never fails to amuse me."

"You think you can get her?"

"Getting her isn't the problem, Gori. Getting her to Red Eyes without his sister spoiling the goods is the problem."

* * *

The seat of House Ireton, Scarborough Castle, was arrayed more for festive celebration than military operation. The presence of Countess Gabriela Robin laid a glamor upon both the castle and its staff. Hosts and staff alike paused as they saw her in her emerald-green dress, matching eyes and fire-red hair flowing as she walked the halls to the chamber reserved for her and her entourage. The noblewoman's voice echoed through the halls, reinforcing the spell, as she and her entourage prepared for a command performance.

While the Duchess oversaw the staff in decorating the Grand Hall and preparing for the festivities, the Countess and her companions rehearsed in a room off to one side. A shadow flashed through the room, and one of the Countess's ladies gasped. "A Solar Guard ship! Everyone, come look!"

Gabriela nodded her assent and the company took a break to gaze out the window as *Baden-Powell* landed at the military spaceport below. Lady Olga drew a pair of binoculars from a bag, hoping to get a clearer look.

"Hey," she said, "do any of you have a heraldry index handy?"

A dandy young man waved a tablet before the group. "Of course, I do", he said. "I am always prepared."

Olga giggled. "Of course, Sir Conte. Come here and look then."

Conte alighted to the window, and he took the binoculars from his colleague. "Olga," he said, "take this and bring up the Solar Guard crests."

Olga traded with Conte and brought up the Guard's library of crests on the tablet. "Ready."

"That's a *Longboat*-class cutter", Conte said, and Olga immediately removed from her search the ships of the line, the battleships that made the Guard as famous as it was formidable. She removed the escorts, the destroyers and cruisers. Last she removed the support vessels, leaving scouts and similar vessels. The unique entries remaining showed vessels belonging to the Star Knights.

"Find one with a lion", Conte said.

"This is it, Conte." Olga said, showing him the ship on the tablet. He looked at it, peered back through the binoculars, and turned to Gabrella.

"My lady, come to the window. The Lord has heard your prayers."

Gabriela took the binoculars from Sir Conte and trained them on the ship. A boy debarked first, then a middle-aged bearded man, and then a tall clean-cut man in the prime of his life. He surveyed the spaceport before looking up to the castle and meeting her gaze. She gasped in surprise, lost his fine features until her companions' giggling broke the spell. She fanned her flushed cheeks.

"Our lady is smitten!" Conte said, "The glory of Lord Roland's visage has made a girl of our noble lady."

Gabriela swatted Conte on the arm. "All right then, back to rehearsal!"

Conte and Olga shared a giggle as they followed Gabriela back to their work, the others following, and soon they again filled the halls with song.

* * *

Duke Ireton was sitting behind his desk in the Master's Chambers, paperwork and screens about him, when the gaunt face of his chamberlain appeared on his monitor. "What is it, Gerald?"

"Your Grace, Lord Roland is here."

The aging master of the Dire March rose from his chair. "Admit our most noble guest." Moments later Ireton's chamber doors opened. Ramsey, Sibley, and little Creton came forth into his presence.

Ireton met Ramsey halfway and shook his hand. "Welcome to the Dire March, Lord Roland. Duke Michael's message impressed me with an urgency I'd not seen from the Church in some time."

"Indeed, Your Grace," Ramsey said.

Ireton nodded towards the doors, and they closed without a word. Once the lock engaged, the Duke spoke. "We are secure. Speak, Lord Roland."

Ramsey gestured to Creton, who produced a tablet from a satchel at his hip and handed it to him. "My man, my page, and I resolved the matter at Garmil's Gate recently. We not only dealt with the pirate problem, Your Grace. We came upon a deeper reason for the Red Eyes Pirates preying upon commercial shipping."

"The Mining Guild?" Ireton said, "I've been having some issues with them of late."

Ramsey held the tablet flat in one hand while activating it with the other. A hologram of a sensory deprivation chamber rose from the tablet's surface.

"While there was a Guild problem, it is this that brought me out here, Your Grace."

"What am I looking at?"

"Your Grace is looking at a suspended animation tank, used for prisoners that cannot be executed, but must be isolated and neutralized."

Sibley followed Ramsey. "As Your Grace sees plainly, this tank is not for men. It is intended for creatures larger in stature than any man, yet not for an animal or other beast."

Ireton stroked the beard upon his chin. "A giant." Ireton said, "Nephilim?"

Worse, Your Grace', Ramsey said, "It held a fallen angel, the worst of those who fathered the Nephlim."

The old duke's eyes grew wide as recognition dawned on him. "The Warforger."

Sibley's voice betrayed no fear. "The most cunning of Red Eyes's henchmen, Dashing Jack, used the entire pirate operation and the Mining Guild's corruption to cover his assault on the planet's hidden prison." Sibley said, "Your Grace, he removed the tank containing the angel before he could be intercepted."

"And the Solar Guard believes that this angel has designs upon my domain?" asked Ireton.

"Not your domain", Ramsey said, "but the treasure it currently hosts. The angel's allegiance would demand a price, a price requiring the finest treasures in all the realms of Mankind."

Still stroking his beard, Ireton said "I see. What shall we do?"

"First", Ramsey said, "I recommend that Your Grace should pray that we are not too late."

"Of course." Ireton said, "When does the Guard expect the raid to come?"

"Our worst case has the raid coming in the next 12 hours." Ramsey said, "Our best case is a day."

"The Lord Marshall needs to be briefed." Ireton said.

"Sibley can handle that." Ramsey said, "I will contact my superiors and report   to   them."

2 GREEN BIRD

Redalen's Revenge approached the abandoned mining colony of Dara's Folly, using its compliment of *Hobgoblin*-class mecha to scout out a path. These ovoid-shaped pods with chicken-like legs, red mono-eyes and cannons attached were as ugly as the men at their controls, but they got the job done.

"I'm glad we only need to skulk through this asteroid field once." Gori said, "After this point in the operation, detection won't matter, not for us."

"Incoming transmission from the Folly." the Communications Officer said.

"Main screen", Jack said. The viewscreen showed a thin gaunt man with severe features.

"Captain Jack, I presume?" the gaunt man said.

"I am", Jack answered. "You're the courier from our man inside, yes?"

"I do. I am Sir Lee, Keeper of the Ducal Seal. I await you within the colony. Dock inside, Captain. Ireton's patrols comb through the belt."

The screen went back to the view of the asteroid belt outside the ship, and *Revenge* arrived at Dara's Folly soon thereafter. She berthed in the open docking bay, left open when the last ship had fled years ago. Gori accompanied Jack to the meeting with the courier while their mecha concealed themselves nearby to watch for Ireton patrols. The two pirates soon entered what was once the operations center of the colony, where Sir Lee and a tall bodyguard awaited them.

"Greetings, Captain." Sir Lee said, "This is my bodyguard, Samson."

Jack   gestured   to   Gori.   "My   executive   officer,   Gori."

Sir Lee nodded, and Samson followed suit.

"The preparations your master asked for are in place", Sir Lee said. "You have what I asked for?"

Gori placed an ornate wooden box on the table between them. "Exactly so." Jack said, "With the High Admiral's compliments."

Samson took the box into his gloved hands. They lit up, initiating a scan that read out on a bracer worn on Samson's shield arm. Once finished, he handed it to Sir Lee, who opened the package and smiled. Within it was a Red Eyes insignia, the size of a lapel pin.

"Remember to wear that pin when the time comes" Gori said, "It will let the others to know to spare you."

"Indeed", Sir Lee said. "Now, to current concerns. There's been a development."

Samson activated the table. A holographic display of *Baden-Powell* rose up from its surface. "This Solar Guard vessel arrived early this morning", Sir Lee said. "It's master came straight from the Council of Stars on Earth, on a matter of importance so severe that I was not privy to it."

"Lord Roland", Jack said. "I didn't expect to see him again so soon. This complicates things."

"It greatly complicates things, Captain. Your target is infatuated with the Star Knight."

Gori and Jack shared a look. "Oh no, it changes the details, but not the plan overall", Jack said with a laugh. "We'll just have to make removing Roland the top tactical objective, instead of giving old Duke Ireton the run-around."

Sir Lee waved. "No, that part I have already guaranteed. I can tie the Duke down with procedure and administration."

"Then I have only Lord Roland to deal with, and I know how to do so, but for that I need to wait for the Vice Admiral to arrive."

Sir Lee cocked an eyebrow. "Vice Admiral?"

* * *

Red Eyes sat upon the skull-adorned throne in the spacious feast hall of the pirate warlord's asteroid fortress: Hell's Heart. A humpbacked cripple scurried to his side from a door nearby.

"Master, the Painbringer awaits."

Without deigning to look in the toady's direction, Red Eyes waved his arm. "Come forth, Vice Admiral."

The doors at the far end opened, and in strode the female reflection of Red Eyes: Zuzu the Painbringer. She was a head or so shorter than Red Eyes, but shared her brother's bold blue skin, blood-red eyes, and flowing red mane of hair. The cripple scurried away as fast as his misshapen limbs allowed, leaving the two alone in the hall.

"Report, Sister."

"The fleet is ready." Zuzu said as she brought up nearby viewscreens, "Construction of the carriers is complete, and we've loaded each with a wing of Goblins. Jack reports that he's contacted our man on New Edinburgh."

"And the advanced party?"

"They are at Dara's Folly. Phase Two of the operation is well underway and will be complete presently."

"And the new unit? How does it run?"

Zuzu grinned. "Better than anything we've ever stolen, including Jack's personal mech. I look forward to testing *Anakim* in combat."

Red Eyes brought up a hologram of the new mech from the projector mounted in his throne. "If Jack's report from the Garmil's Gate operation is accurate, *Anakim* should be sufficient to handle any unexpected enemies."

"Or expected ones", Zuzu added. "Jack also reports that Lord Roland is on New Edinburgh."

Red Eyes laughed. "That cunning bastard! You know what he means by reporting this to me, Sister?"

Zuzu shook her head.

"He's well aware that he cannot confront the Star Knight again so soon", Red Eyes said. "He's throwing that problem back to me, and that means it's going to be up to you to deal with Roland. How do you propose to make him come away from our prize so that Jack can snatch it out from under their noses?"

Zuzu pondered her response for a moment. Then she showed her plan on a viewscreen. "If the first wave of asteroids is sufficient to lock down Ireton's orbital forces, would we not be able to jump right on the edge of the gravity well and then make a dive for Scarborough Castle and the surrounding town?"

Red Eyes switched the display to an image of New Edinburgh. "Even at best speed, we can only count on a few thousand asteroids, and those need to be flung right at the core colonies here at Lagrange 2, where the Duke's docks are. Forcing Ireton to defend his fleet in dry dock will require sending every ship and mech he's got, but that won't be enough."

"Why not?"

"Because the plan relies on Ireton's familiarity with natural asteroid swarms. They're practiced at shooting them into harmless pieces. The point of weaponizing these asteroids is to buy time for the next wave to get into position."

Zuzu nodded. "Ah, that's when the fleet attacks in strength!"

"Exactly!" Red Eyes said, "Ireton's forces will be damaged and engaged when we come at them on the far side--here, at Lagrange 4--which will be undefended at first. Lay waste to those colonies, sack them for all they're worth, and don't worry about the Goblins."

The siblings' laughter filled the hall.

"Six thousand of them? All at once?" Zuzu said. "There's no way the colony defenses can handle that many. We're guaranteed to overwhelm all of them there, and woe to the fools that try to stop us!"

"Indeed. The sheer numbers we're throwing at them will horrify them."

"And the surface?"

"You're correct about jumping close-in and diving for the castle, Sister" Red Eyes said. "But leave that to Jack. Link up with *Revenge*. She will be fresh, and their Hobgoblins will stand up better to Ireton's Gallowglass units. In addition, our man on the inside has a surprise waiting for the castle's garrison. That surprise should keep them, as well as Lord Roland, busy long enough for you and Jack to finish the job."

"And what of Jack?"

"He will have his own egress planned, and I am certain he already expects to use it. Don't worry about him. Just ensure that Phase Three concludes as planned and be certain to execute Phase Four before returning to base."

Zuzu saluted her brother. "For the Glory of Babylon!"

Red Eyes smiled. "Your command awaits, Sister. Do me proud."

Zuzu turned about and strutted away. As the doors to the hall closed behind her, Red Eyes cackled. "You shall have your prize yet, Azazel."

* * *

Countess Gabriela Robin strode at speed across the Grand Hall, and her cousin Count Vikuun Qis followed right behind. "Cousin!" he said, "Lord Roland has vital duties to perform. You cannot just approach him unannounced!"

"Vikky, he has to eat or drink sometime. I am free to approach him then." Gabriella replied, "No one will care if a lady is seen approaching a lord with the intent to feed him."

They left the Grand Hall and turned towards the kitchen. "Do you intend to bring his food to him like a common maid?" Vikuun said.

Gabriela waved him off. "Why not? Plenty of epic romances began when the heroine went for the man she desired."

"You read far too many such romances, Cousin", Vikkun said. "The reality is far different. Have you never read the Qis family archives?"

She mocked him with a false yawn. "All that begetting puts me to sleep, Vikky. You speak like a bitter old man. It's unbecoming of a young man of your quality. Did you never hear the command to bring a joyful noise?"

"Gabby, when I am not obligated to oversee your security, I spend far too much time aiding our fathers in the work of our domains, especially looking after our interests in the Court of Stars on Earth. I am fortunate to hear joy, apart from when I am with you, only in fleeting moments at St. Paul's during

Mass."

"You need to lament less and celebrate more, Cousin", Gabriela said.

"You, Cousin, need to consider that Star Knights don't appear someplace for no reason. He is not here to satisfy your romantic desires. He is here to fulfill his duty."

An aide approached the pair, bowed and said, "Count Qis, you are commanded to answer a call from Earth."

He sighed. "See, Gabby?"

Her face softened, and she put a hand on his cheek. "I am sorry for being so difficult, Cousin. I know you're being true and faithful to my father. I will not seek out trouble." She gave him on the cheek. "Go, Cousin. Do your duty."

Reluctantly, Count Qis turned away and exited down the hall. The aide left with him. Gabriela waited until both men were out of sight, and then she turned back towards the kitchen. "He has nothing to worry about", she said to herself with a mischievous grin, "but Lord Roland might."

* * *

Gabriela found Sir Ramsey as he exited the Armory. She followed from a distance until Ramsey entered the Keep where the ducal quarters were. She saw him enter one of the guest chambers, one across from her own. She knew that there were empty guest quarters in the Keep, so it stood to reason that a Star Knight would be lodged there. She spotted Creton emerging from a lift down the hall with a satchel over his shoulder. She locked eyes with the boy, put up a finger to hush him with one hand, and waved him closer with the other. Stunned, Creton complied.

"You are Lord Roland's page." she whispered, "What did he send you for?"

"A loaf of bread and some tea", Creton replied.

"Give it to me. I will deliver it", Gabriela said. She snatched the bag off the boy's shoulder in a smooth motion. Before he could object, she bounded out the doorway and entered Ramsey's quarters without so much as a word to announce her.

Not that Ramsey needed it. "It's been a while since a girl thought herself so clever as to play highwayman to my page."

Gabriela stood across the table from him as she spread the sachel's bounty upon it. "When was my lord's last time taking a meal with a woman?"

Ramsey laughed. "Before leaving Earth. Sibley's wife cooked a fine dinner at Christmas."

"My lord's sergeant-at-arms is blessed with a good wife", Gabriela said as she cut the bread, "but he himself is not."

"My lady is well-acquainted with what is said in coffee houses and salons throughout Christendom, but I am curious to hear who among her entourage wants to retire by marrying me. I cannot believe that my lady would want to surrender this life of travel for the daily duties of hearth and home."

Creton approached. "I am sorry, my lord. I don't know how-"

"Come here, boy." Ramsey said with a chuckle, "No harm done, so no foul. If anything, I should fault my lady here for being so brazen with her powers. Take some bread for yourself and take some down to the Armory for your father to tide him over until we dine tonight."

Creton's face lit up, and off he raced on his errand. "You already have a paternal touch", Gabreila said.

"The boy's been my page for three years now. One has to acquire fatherly ways to successfully make a boy into a knight."

"Yet his father serves you also."

"For now, until Creton can bear arms in his own right as a squire. Then Sibley can retire, and by then he will have earned it."

"And once Creton too is a knight?"

"Does my lady fear for my soul, that I might die of loneliness?"

"I fear that my lord would sin by shunning love willingly offered when he need not."

"My lady calls 'love' something less reliable than my arms and vessel," Ramsey said. "I would not shun it if it were so reliable."

Gabreila took his arm. "At least I can rely on my lord to speak truth to me."

"But do you hear it?" Ramsey said, smiling.

Gabriela smiled back. "Better than my lord may think."

* * *

Count Vikuun stood watching the encounter between Gabriela and Ramsey from a hacked security feed when a bell rang out. He drew a palm-sized holographic projector from his vest and put it on a desk nearby. As the image materialized, he put up his hood, drew his cloak about himself, and adjusted the cloak pin at his neck.

"Speak, High Admiral", Vikuun said, his voice distorted.

The image stabilized. It was Red Eyes, kneeling in thrall to him.

"Master, the plan to raid New Edinburgh and take Countess Robin for Azazel is ready. Only one difficulty arose: The Solar Guard is aware of Azazel's return to the galaxy and has dispatched Lord Roland to the planet to confer with Duke Ireton."

"He is not the problem you believe him to be. Proceed with the operation as planned. Lord Roland shall be dealt with."

Red Eyes did not immediately reply.

"Have you something to say, High Admiral?"

"Master, should I not adjust the plan?"

"I shall handle the matter, High Admiral. Proceed as planned."

"Phase One is complete as I speak. Phase Two is underway. Phase Three shall be ready as planned."

"Commence the attack as soon as you are ready, High Admiral. Our partner will not be satisfied without payment in full. Don't keep him waiting."

"Understood, Master. Victory for Babylon!"

"Victory for Babylon!"

The image winked out, and Vikuun put the projector away immediately. As he looked out at the flirting between his cousin and his enemy, Vikuun pondered his options.

I could assassinate Roland here and now, Vikuun thought, but doing so would cause more problems than it would solve. No, during the attack would be the best opportunity to see the deed done, as it would easily be attributed to the chaos of the battle. That gives plausible deniability, and that is my only route to removing him successfully.

Vikuun took one more look at Gabriela and Ramsey smiling at each other before he turned away from the scene entirely. *Now to clear the way for Baron Sheelak again.* Vikuun thought, and he left the tower room to arrange to get Dashing Jack's alter-ego to pass security that night.

3 SWORDS & FLOWERS

Zuzu the Painbringer led a massive carrier group from the bridge of her flagship *Great Gomorrah*. The carriers and their cruiser and battleship escorts burst out of hyperspace at the edge of the New Edinburgh system. They followed the same path towards Dara's Folly as Dashing Jack but halted at the edge of the asteroid belt. Zuzu turned to the ship's captain, who had called up a holographic display of the operations map.

"Ma'am", the Captain said, "the mining crews report that they'd finished selecting asteroids out of the belt and weaponizing them. They just need drivers. The mecha wings aboard the ships of the fleet all reported being in good order, and their pilots sober and in order. The ships reported all systems nominal, and the boarding parties were ready to deploy."

"It's exciting, isn't it?" Zuzu said. "This is the biggest raid we've ever conducted."

"Aye, it is." The Captain's voice didn't sound so convincing.

"But?" Zuzu crossed her arms.

"Everything has to unfold exactly as the High Admiral said it will, Ma'am." The Captain said, "If we lose the element of surprise, then we're lucky if we die screaming under Ireton guns."

"And if we're not so lucky?"

"First we're excommunicated. Then we're hanged."

"So far everything is unfolding as predicted, Captain", Zuzu said. "What could go wrong?"

"The Solar Guard could intervene, Ma'am."

"Already accounted for, Captain." Zuzu said, "The High Admiral has accounted for even the most severe intervention. Now get me on the line."

"You heard the Vice Admiral." The Captain said to his Communications Officer, and moments later she was on with the whole fleet.

"This is Vice Admiral Zuzu", she said. "Before us lies Dara's Folly, the trap unto which we shall draw the Iretons to their doom. We shall now execute the next phase of the operation. Each ship shall hold here until further notice. Insubordination shall be punished by summary execution, done in the High Admiral's name. That is all."

The comlink cut out. "Captain, is *Anakim* ready?"

"No, Ma'am. You'll have to take a Goblin to the rendezvous."

"Not even one of the new variants?"

"All assigned to the battleships, Ma'am."

Her face frowned. "If I need to punch someone later, you had better hope I don't think to use you as the bag." She stomped off to the lift. The Captain sighed, and once the lift doors closed he keyed the comlink again.

"Hangar Bay here."

"She's on her way, Chief", the Captain said, "Warm up a Goblin and be nice about it. She's mad about Anakim."

"Understood Bridge," the Hanger Chief said. "We'll get her out as fast as we can."

Moments later the captain of Great Gomorrah silently watched Zuzu's Goblin surge forth to make the meeting at Dara's Folly.

* * *

Creton entered the Armory of Scarborough Castle, where he found his father Sibley and Duke Ireton's Lord Marshall Sir Thomas Gibson, standing over a table displaying holographic images. A guard followed the boy in.

"My lords, Lord Roland's page."

Creton bowed. "My lord dispatched me to my father." he said, handing his father bread and tea.

"None for me?" Sir Thomas said with a laugh, "Don't take that rebuke seriously my boy. Your master could not know."

"Indeed." Sibley said as he pulled a stool to the table, "Come, Son. Now's a good time to learn from your elders."

Sir Thomas gave the old warrior a knowing nod, and as Creton stood on the stool to get a better look over the table the old knight continued. "This 'Goblin' design shocked everyone at the Court of Stars.'

"Is this new, my lord?" Creton blurted in his curiosity.

"It is, lad" Sir Thomas said, "Brand new pirate design, I don't think you saw these when you went to Garmil's Gate with your father and your master."

Creton saw a crude box using a single sensor eye, lacking arms, with chicken-style legs attached and a pair of blaster cannons fixed forward. The legs and feet had thrusters, as did the aft of the box where the cockpit and engines were. The combination of eye and cannons created the image of a face, a mockery of a face. "It doesn't look like much. *Durendal* could crush them by stepping on them."

Sibley and Thomas laughed. "It's a machine for savages and degenerates, boy." Sibley said, "These pirates spawn without love, kill without reason, and die without purpose. It's a perfect machine for such wretches. They're cheap to make and easy to use. The threat comes from their numbers, and then in how fast you can replace them."

"Wait," Creton said. "If they stole their mecha before, but now they make them, why do they make what they used to steal?"

"That's a good question, my boy." Sir Thomas smiled. "The answer is what worries all of us. They also stole the ships they used. Are they now making those also? We know they can, and do, often hollow out asteroids as supply dumps and rest stations. If they can do that, then-"

"- why not make ships out of them?" Creton said.

"Your son has a point, Master Sibley." Sir Thomas said as he left the room. "I must make a call."

"Did I say something wrong?" Creton asked his father.

"No, Son. You said something right, and it was something he hadn't thought of before now."

Thomas came back into the room. "There, that should soon satisfy the question."

"How?" Creton let his face show his confusion.

"I dispatched a cruiser to the belt." Sir Thomas said. "The only source of asteroids near here is Dara's Folly. If there's any chance that you're on the right track, we'll find out soon enough. In the meantime, I released an advisory to watch for asteroid storms in the coming days."

"Sound thinking, my lord." Sibley said. "Remember this, Son. Panic is as fatal as any foe. Before I have you wield steel in your hand, you've got to have steel about your heart!"

Thomas continued. "By putting the garrisons on alert for a storm, I get them ready to protect the habitats without giving them cause to fear. If it turns out to be nothing, then they can stand down and no harm is done. If it bears out, then they're in place to face the threat and more likely to do so properly."

* * *

Zuzu landed her Goblin inside the docking bay of Dara's Folly, and when she joined Jack and Sir Lee she did not hide her foul mood.

"You lot had better be ready to move, because I'm ready to beat someone to death."

"We await one more element, and then we are free to depart." Jack said, "If you're as punctual as usual then that should arrive right about now."

A klaxon sounded, and a hologram of a hooded man appeared. Everyone in the room knelt before the hologram. "Welcome, Master." Jack said.

"Everyone is present. Good." the hologram said. "Rise. We shall go over the plan one more time."

"One more time." Jack agreed. Gori, Zuzu, Samson, and Sir Lee nodded their concurrence.

"I return on the courier shuttle with Jack, who changes into his disguise as Sheelak." Sir Lee said, "I sweep him through security and into the castle, where he lays out his escape routes before moving on the target. Meanwhile, Gori and Zuzu return to the fleet and begin the attack. The time it will take to return and get into position will be more than enough for Jack and I to return to the castle and make ready the heist."

Jack picked up the thread. "While the attack goes on in orbit, the sabotage measures prepared in the castle go live and throw the place into chaos. This is the signal for Gori to pick up Zuzu and bring *Revenge* down to the castle. Zuzu and *Revenge*'s mecha squadron hold off any defenders while I take the prize and meet Revenge on the roof of the citadel. We take the aft retrieval hatch; I hand the prize to my security team and prepare to assist the escape back into space."

Sir Lee nodded.

"Not even Lord Roland can stop this plan from coming together", Gori said.

"Oh," Sir Lee said, "I have specific measures on hand to stop Lord Roland if he threatens to spoil the plan. We shan't repeat the lessons of Garmil's Gate."

Zuzu grinned. "And if you somehow screw it all up, I will not hesitate to step in and kill Roland for you instead!"

"Your enthusiasm is welcome, Vice Admiral" the hooded man said, "and I hope it is not needed."

"We are all agreed then?" Jack said.

Sir Lee, Gori, Samson, and Zuzu all nodded. The hooded man smiled.

"Victory for Babylon!" the hooded man said.

"Victory for Babylon!" the others answered in unison, and the hologram winked out.

* * *

Ramsey escorted Gabriela into the Grand Hall. Her entourage followed behind them. The Hall's original purpose of being a chamber designed for the holding of court and other occasions of great ceremony and rituals of public importance made it ideal for use as a concert hall. Duchess Ireton called Gabriela over.

"Countess," the Duchess smiled at her, "everything will be ready for your performance after dinner tonight."

Gabriela curtsied. "My company and I are grateful for your hospitality,

Your Grace."

Duchess Ireton turned to Ramsey. "Will my noble lord be her escort tonight?"

"Of course!" Gabreila said hastily, "He came all the way from Earth just to see to my security."

Ramsey bowed. "My lady believes she will perform best if she in my company."

"And Count Qis has no objection?" the Duchess said.

Gabriela again spoke quickly. "He has stated none."

"Then I shall leave this place." Duchess Ireton said, "I must see to the feast's final preparations before evening prayers. Until then."

"Until then." Gabriela curtsied again as the Duchess left.

"Until then." Ramsey bowed. He and Gabriela then moved into the practice room and closed the door behind them.

"My lady is too eager to speak when it favors her." Ramsey said. The playful tone from earlier had gone.

"My lord, you truly think that I am the target of a pirate raid? Even if this is a frontier world, it is still the seat of the Dire March. Our hosts are not fools who use their men-at-arms as players' props. Even if such a raid were to come, what it would take to reach this castle is beyond the most fevered imaginations."

"My lady, I am disappointed. Your father should have told you that when the Solar Guard arrives, we do not enter your world. You enter ours. The only reason I have not already put you and your companions on a ship to Earth is because our intelligence suggests that there is enough time for your performance. Right after that, off you go."

The iron-hard tone hit Gabriela as if she's been struck by hand. "But my lord."

"Enough." Ramsey said, "I am here to do my duty, my lady, and right now that means getting you out of harm's way. If you persist in this behavior, I will cancel your performance and remove you immediately."

Gabriela looked at Ramsey, pleading with her eyes, but she soon found that it wasn't going to bend him to her desire as it has to others. She sighed. "Yes, my lord."

* * *

Samson, Jack, and Sir Lee traveled in Lee's yacht, *Iago*, a customized and refurbished *Foxhound*-class patrol boat. Now fitted for speed and comfort, Sir Lee came and went from New Edinburgh in the manner one expects of Duke Ireton's chief officials. In the lounge-like commons, Jack and Lee sat across the table, while Samson alone handled the ship on the bridge.

"You have had no difficulty coming and going?" Jack asked.

"I have several daughters who now run households throughout the Dire March", Sir Lee said as he poured a drink, "That alone has me traveling frequently. Then there's my duties as Keeper of the Ducal Seal, where I am necessary for certain ceremonial affairs in lieu of the duke himself."

Jack pulled a pen-like device from a sleeve as he watched Lee pour a drink. He twisted a few segments this way and that, then put the pen-like thing on the table.

"His Grace the duke suspects nothing?"

Sir Lee drained his glass. "Of course not. It plays into his pattern of taking his oldest retainers for granted."

"Is that what this is about, for you?"

Sir Lee poured himself another drink. "It seems petty, doesn't it? Yet I had been by the duke's side since he succeeded his father. There had been wars, assassinations, pirate incursions, and revolts all this time. I had many sons once, but they died for the duke, and Ireton did nothing to save my family from extinction. Not once did he offer a daughter to a son of mine. Not once did he offer me foundlings to take as my own. He watched as my family withered and did nothing. I am the last of the line, Jack. Why should I be loyal to a man who could have saved my family, but refused to do so? Why be loyal to that?"

"You would see the house fall to satisfy your need for revenge?"

"Let the duke know my plight. Then, maybe, we can talk repairing the breech."

Jack picked up the pen-like thing and shut it off. "You'll have all you seek soon   enough."

4 TONIGHT COMES A HURRICANE

Zuzu the Painbringer strode across the hangar bay of *Great Gomorrah* with the menace of a lioness on the hunt. Arrayed in racks from floor to ceiling in this warehouse-sized hangar rested artless box-shaped mecha with chicken legs, red mono-eyes, and cannons bolt on the face.

Open hatches on their tops were the only proof that they weren't robots, as those hatches revealed crude cockpits. As she strode by those racks, she checked the seals of her battle armor: a matte black carapace, with a white skull outline on the chest plate and red eyes in the sockets. It hugged her muscled curves as well as it covered her bold blue skin. She looked down at the wing of men she was about to lead into battle, standing a full head taller than the tallest of them, and gave them lewd grins that bared her fangs. They cheered her as she passed.

In the center of the bay knelt a new manlike model with colors and insignia mirroring her armor and a cockpit large enough for her inhuman frame. The rose-mounted cockpit lay open but Zuzu did not immediately mount it. Instead she turned about to face her fellow reavers.

"Red Eyes' Reavers, hear your mistress!" she bellowed. "In a few moments we launch from this ship and sortie in the greatest raid this galaxy has seen in over a century. We do what none dared think possible, stage a direct assault upon the heart of our enemy's territory: House Ireton's home world of New Edinburgh!"

The gathered men roared, their eyes stared in rapt attention and their mouths watered as if anticipating a kill.

"The Iretons are soft and weak! They believe that we cannot reach them where they live and keep their treasures. They plot to seize and conquer more of our land, our worlds, our lives from us in the name of their Duke and their God. They are wrong!"

The men cheered in unison: "Victory for Babylon!"

"Today we show them with blood and fire that they are wrong! We shall crush them, drive them before us, and reap from them all of their treasure- and their God shall avail them not against us!"

"Victory for Babylon!"

"We bring the pain to them! The men that bring me the most heads shall be rewarded with my love!"

"Victory for Babylon!"

"Mount up! We shall wade knee-deep in their blood and seize the greatest treasures in all the galaxy this day. Victory for Babylon!"

"Victory for Babylon!" they cried out in ecstasy as they scrambled into the cockpits of their Goblins. As Zuzu mounted her unit, all the racked mechs in the bay began powering up. One by one the red eyes in the heads lit up, their legs flexed, and they soon resembled a disturbed hive of wasps. Zuzu's unit closed the door to the cockpit and rose to stand.

"Bridge, this is the Painbringer. Ready check."

"All clear, Vice Admiral. We're ready."

"Signal the first wave", Zuzu said. "We're launching."

"Aye, Ma'am", Bridge said. The warning klaxons sounded.

"Reavers, prepare to launch", Zuzu said. Her men released their Goblins from the racks on the hangar bay's walls. Still in Walker mode, the first flight on either side of the bay stood ready to go. The klaxons ceased, the bay depressurized, and the doors opened to space. Four Goblins per side hit their engines and flew out in formation into space. All 60 mecha departed the bay within a minute leaving only Zuzu to go."

"Vice Admiral Zuzu," she said, "*Anakim*, launching!"

Zuzu spun up the engines and blasted off from the hangar bay on the port side. She swerved towards the bow of *Great Gomorrah* and accelerated to catch up to her men. Blazing points streamed on all sides as the fleet's other carriers launched their mecha wings. Soon a great mass of six-thousand Goblin-class mecha melded together into a massive formation, with Zuzu's *Anakim* in the lead.

* * *

The Ireton heavy cruiser *MacCullough* followed the routine patrol route, passing well outside the planetary sphere for orbital traffic and towards Dara's Folly. A flight of *Gallowglass*-class mecha, House Ireton's standard unit, flew alongside the cruiser as a Combat Space Patrol, connecting as required to refuel and swap pilots. The Gallowglass units, compared to *MacCullough*'s three-hundred-meter length and sixty meter height, gave the image of four giant soldiers escorting the cruiser.

On the bridge, the viewscreen changed to show one of the Gallowglass pilots. "Flight Leader to Bridge", he said, "I'm advancing on the sensor contact now."

"Acknowledged, Flight Leader", the Captain said.

The lead mecha flew far ahead of *MacCullough*. Soon it was well out of visual range of the cruiser, and within visual range of the sensor contact. First a blip, then a few, then more, and more, and more of them. Thousands of discreet contacts filled the pilot's head's-up display, all of them approach fast on course for New Edinburgh.

"Flight Leader to Bridge", the pilot said, "we have an asteroid swarm coming, a big one. Thousands of them."

The Captain turned to his Communications Officer. "Open a line to New Edinburgh. The Lord Marshal needs to be informed."

The pilot fired the unit's vernier thrusters and maneuvered above the swarm's plane. His sensors now had visual lock on the leading edge of the swarm, and he saw that these asteroids weren't moving on their own, but instead had rockets attached. As he reopened his comlink with *MacCullough*, he saw that something--that someone--had targeted him.

"*MacCullough*!" he yelled as he tried to evade missiles launched at him from the asteroids, "Those aren't errant asteroids. They've got rockets installed."

"Oh God." the Captain said as he watched the video feed from the flight leader, "Comms, do we have that link yet?"

"No, sir!" the Communications Officer said, "We're being jammed."

The viewscreen showed a massive shower of asteroids, each the size of *MacCullough*, closing on their position at high speed.

"Evasive action!" the Captain said, "Keep trying to contact Headquarters."

The cruiser turned on its axis to speed away on the vertical from the wave closing on them, going--in effect--over the storm. The other Gallowglass mecha surged forward to rescue their leader. On the screen a second window with one of the Gallowglass pilots appeared.

"Captain, those asteroids are armed! They're are hostile ships!" the pilot said.

"We're in weapons range, Captain!" the Tactical Officer said.

"Fire!" the Captain said, and *MacCullough*'s guns fired at each target in range, destroying each in turn, but it was just enough to keep from getting hit. *MacCullough* kept firing as she rose above the storm, trying to get clear of the enemy's jamming.

"New contacts to port!" the Sensors Officer said, "Missiles! We're being targeted directly!"

"Counter-battery fire!" the Captain said, "Helm, get us out of here!

MacCullough's point-defense guns shot down the missiles as they approached, buying time for the cruiser to turn about, but *Redalen's Revenge* emerged from hyperspace directly above *MacCullough* at optimal range for her guns. A volley of fire from its bow-facing turrets pierced the ship's shields and lanced the Ireton cruiser's hull. One shot pierced *MacCullough*'s missile magazine, exploding all the ordinance at once, annihilating the Ireton heavy cruiser in a massive fireball that consumed all hands. Without a mothership, the flight of Gallowglass mecha succumbed soon after.

"*Revenge* to *Great Gomorrah*", Gori said as his blue-skinned face smugly grinned from ear to ear, "Obstacle cleared. Losses minimal. Surprise maintained."

* * *

Jack met Count Qis in the latter's chambers in Scarborough Castle.

"Sheelak," Qis said feigning gaiety as he shook Jack's hand, "it is good to see you friend. Your errands afield concluded well?"

"Better than I expected, my lord."

Qis waved away his attendants. "We require privacy." The handful of servants left the room, and Qis barred the door behind them. He drew forth a disc the size of a coin from a pocket. With a flick of his wrist, it began to hum. Qis put it on a table.

"We may speak freely now."

Jack knelt before Qis. "All proceeds as you instructed. The Red Eyes Armada is ready to strike."

"Rise", Qis said, his voice now grave with an otherworldly menace. "The work of our forefathers remains undone."

"But with the return of the first of the Watchers to the galaxy-"

"We try again what was thwarted a millennium ago."

"And this current matter?"

"Proof of concept, Sheelak. It does not matter how it ends. We are already victorious. It is now only a matter of discovering what specifics require our attention as we move our plan forward."

"And Azazel knows this?"

"Without question. All that needs be done is to pass him a token to let him know when to escape."

"As for the current matter?"

"Only the household, their sworn vassals, and certain trusted others shall be permitted here in the ducal quarters when that time comes. You shall secret yourself herein and hide, as Jack. Once the ladies retreat here, come forth and take our prize. By the time anyone could possibly interfere, counter-measures shall be in place to ensure your success."

Qis retrieved a box from a footlocker. "After reviewing your performance at Garmil's Gate, I deemed it necessary to increase your persona's infamy."

Jack took the box and opened it. Inside he found a half-mask with red lenses in the eye sockets. "Dashing indeed, master."

"Put them on."

Jack donned the mask, and he saw a user interface light up before his eyes.

In his field of vision, he saw options to open a data link, a readout of a scan on Count Qis before him showing that his master concealed a beam sword up one sleeve, and other functions as if he were using a tablet.

"Now your persona is complete, my friend" Qis said. "Your infamy shall surpass the great villains of old."

Jack turned to look into the mirror. He brushed his fair blond hair out of his face. "Yes, this will do nicely."

"It will also give you the edge you will need against enemies like Lord Roland. The artificers and programmers of Kuroyama take pride in their craftsmanship."

Jack saw a text message from Zuzu pop up in the corner of his vision: "We are coming. Stand ready."

"The attack is imminent." Jack said.

"Then the key feature works. Good. I will rely on that comlink in the days to come", Qis said. "Thus concludes our audience. I must go attend the performance now."

"How to explain Baron Sheelak's absence?" Jack said.

"Delayed by family business too urgent to ignore."

The men shared a laugh. Qis retrieved his privacy device and led Sheelak back to Gabriela's chambers. There Sheelak changed into his pirate garb, became Dashing Jack once more and took a seat away from the door. Qis descended to the Grand Hall for a performance fated to not finish.

* * *

"Our honored guest shall now perform for us!" Duke Ireton said.

Rather than take up a stage or fill out an arena, His Grace the Duke had arranged for a much smaller and more intimate gathering by moving all the tables in the Grand Hall into a rough, broken circle. Gabriela stepped forth into that makeshift theater in the round. Her chief players--Lady Olga and Lord Conte--followed. She spotted Ramsey hurrying back into the Grand Hall to take a seat near the citadel door. His man Sibley joined Ramsey, and young Creton also. A warmth of familial sentiment prompted one of her joyful, playful smiles.

Gabriela's cousin, Count Vikuun Qis, entered through the same door as Ramsey and resumed his seat at table. Her smile remained, but the feeling faded. Something about her distaff relation always struck her as slightly amiss. The man she'd seen Vikuun with earlier, Baron Sheelak, was absent but Gabriela dismissed the thought with a shake of her head. She brushed her fire-red hair from her shoulders. She addressed her host.

"Most gracious Duke and Duchess Ireton, my noble friends and I are humbled by your command to play for you tonight."

The Duke and Duchess rose from their chairs. "We are pleased that you have come as called, Countess. Our domain was once a wilderness, tamed and civilized by fierce men and faithful hearts. Those days are ending now. Soon the Dire March shall be no more, and in its place shall be a new civilized domain. We can now join our fellow men in making beautiful what was formerly foul. We call you forth to begin that transformation, a deed witnessed far beyond this chamber tonight."

"My friends and I are honored to be the ones to mark the taming of a frontier." Gabriela said.

Now Ireton continued. "To ensure that all the hearts of our people be reached, we shall share your performance throughout our domain as it happens. All of the Dire March may look on from afar, hearing as we hear and seeing as we see, by ducal decree."

Gabriela gasped as she realized the implication. Tens of millions would watch her this night.

"Then, Your Grace, let us begin."

"Play on." Duke Ireton said. That order prompted the broadcast to begin, and soon crowds large and small gathered across the planet and in its many colonies. Some met in private homes. Some met in pubs. Public transports played the broadcast on their cars, busses, trains, or shuttles. As the signal reached the FTL repeaters, that audience spread across the galaxy and the process repeated itself. Before Gabriela started the show, all the galaxy gave her their undivided attention.

Gabriela pecked Ramsey on the cheek and then flitted back to the center of her makeshift stage. "Tonight, I tell a tale of old, a tale first told in song, the tale of a fighting man and the princess he went to war for. Come with me back across the ages, to a time before the Cataclysm, to a tale of a knight-errant of Old Earth and a princess of a Mars as red and dusky as she who reigned over it."

Sir Conte, on the guitar, struck a dramatic chord. Lady Olga harmonized with Conte's accompaniment. With eyes on Ramsey, Gabriela began to sing. She took up the role of the Martian princess, and she sang a long lament of her kingdom's decline. She sang of treacherous nobles and their intrigues with her enemies. As Her Martian Majesty, Gabriela sang the tale of a lady that suffered until she came to her wits' end and cried out for deliverance.

Conte, taking up the Knight's role, sang of despair at defeat in a war against a cruel empire. He went west in search of a cause as worthy as that he fought for, and as he seemed to find his fate at the hands of foul savages he found deliverance in a cave.

All the room sat rapt in the of the performance, except for Ramsey and Qis. Ramsey showed his appreciation with a bright smile. Qis seemed to have his mind elsewhere.

* * *

Alarm klaxons sounded throughout Lagrange 2. Every colony's garrison reported to battle stations. All the pilots mounted their Gallowglass units and stood ready to launch. The Ireton navy on station formed up and launched their own Gallowglass units. Civilian traffic fled for the other points, left the system, or descended into the atmosphere to escape the coming asteroid storm. As the ships spread out to maximize firepower, forming into a thin curtain wall between the asteroid swarm and those many orbital habitats, the asteroids seemed to mirror their movements. The senior officer on duty at L2 was one of Duke Ireton's sons, Count Henry Ireton, and he did not fail to notice the oddity before him.

But Count Ireton did not change procedure. First, he ordered missiles in volleys, massive volleys tens of thousands in number, be launched at the swarm. Some warheads found their mark and vaporized an asteroid. Others got shot down by blaster cannons, and that got the officers and crew concerned. The Gallowglass units converged on the swarm from all sides in a perfect cylindrical formation, as successive missile volleys flew down the virtual corridor. They opened fire with their beam rifles, only for the swarm to return fire with missiles and blaster cannons. The swarm closed with the fleet. Naval guns reduced the numbers rushing them, but not enough. Asteroid pilots began deliberately ramming the Ireton fleet.

Ireton's formation broke, and the swarm continued on to the orbital installations. The Ireton forces turned to pursue at top speed. They continued to wear away at the swarm, but the sheer number soon had the officers in a panic and they called for aide. As the asteroids closed, more Ireton vessels arrived from the other Lagrange points in orbit and joined the fray. Many more vessels got rammed in turn, but wave after wave of reinforcements winnowed the swarm until only a fraction remained. The habitats' own mecha and guns ensured that those who broke through to connect were very few and far between.

The Ireton vessels regrouped outside of the chief colony of LaGrange 2, where the orbital docks were for Ireton's fleet. They tallied their losses in men and material. The Lord Marshall, Sir Thomas, at Scarborough Castle got the after-action report: Two thousand vessels, with a combined total of ten-thousand mecha, had engaged the swarm. They lost a tenth with all hands, with another 20% damaged and unable to fight. 40% of their mecha was lost or damaged. Five colonies got breeched and took casualties, with a handful of fatalities each, but no vital systems lost and only supplies disrupted due to damage sustained.

* * *

Zuzu the Painbringer kept track of the Ireton response to the asteroid attack on one monitor while keeping Gabriela's concert on another. She sent a signal to the Goblin horde behind her and they changed course to advance upon Lagrange 4. The warships in her wake followed her lead. Now she had a timetable to maximize her opportunity. Between the response to the asteroids and the beaming of the concert, she knew exactly when she had to hit to achieve maximum impact.

Zuzu kept an ear on the concert feed as she advanced upon the leading colony. Her display tracked the distance to target. She adjusted *Anakim*'s speed to match up the tempo of Gabriela's song, knowing that most of the colonial militia on station were paying attention to the concert instead of their sensors.

"*Anakim* to *Revenge*."

Gori's smiling face appeared on her display. "Yes, Vice Admiral."

"Take the cruisers and enact envelopment when I move in with the Goblin horde. Delay launching your mecha until enemy relief arrives."

"Understood, Ma'am", Gori said. "I will signal you when it's time to descend."

Zuzu's display informed her that she'd reached the mark to engage. "All units accelerate to combat speed. For the glory of Babylon!"

The Red Eyes units accelerated on command, launching a massive wave of missiles at the colony cluster of Lagrange 4 just as Countess Gabriela's song reached its climax. Zuzu saw that the Ireton garrisons didn't fire upon their missiles until the wave cleared half the distance to target. She figured that the haphazard, disorganized firing by the colony defense cannons panicked many of the gunners. She watched as her Goblins closed into dogfighting range. They outnumbered the defending Gallowglass units four or more to one. Those hapless Gallowglass pilots that sortied at all got shot to pieces.

Zuzu and a few Goblins descended upon the nearest colony and skimmed its surface from stem to stern, destroying turrets on the hull. The Goblins made full use of the disorganization to annihilate the Gallowglass squadrons before the militia could recover from the confusion.

Zuzu saw that all capacity for resistance at Lagrange 4 had now collapsed. Zuzu got on the line and said, "Loot and pillage, my Goblins!"

Now on the inside, the Goblins swarmed through every Lagrange 4 colony. They found the wealth in the colonies--raw materials, foodstuffs, data, security clearances, arms--and took them to the waiting holds of the cruisers now in the docking bays as well as the few civilian transports found in those bays.

Zuzu stood in the bay of the lead colony, her cockpit open, and cackled manically as she tossed a civilian operator's lifeless corpse into space. "We've gutted them. We've slaughtered them. We are knees-deep in Ireton blood. What glorious slaughter!"

"*Revenge* to *Anakim*." Gori's voice filled her helmet, "It's time."

"On my way!"

Zuzu sealed her cockpit. Moments later she emerged from a side passage and rendezvoused with Revenge, which had already set course for the surface of New Edinburgh. Revenge's aft ventral retrieval ramp laid open and extended for her. She easily caught up and landed Anakim on the flight deck.

As the ramp retracted and closed, a crewman approached. "Do you need anything, ma'am?"

As she emerged from her mecha, she saw Jack's own unit, a stolen black-and-red *Cataphract*-class mech, resembling its historical namesake, dubbed *Black Knight*, across the deck.

"Top off the ordnance." Zuzu said, and then continued, "Why is the Captain's unit here?"

"His orders, Ma'am. More than that I don't know. Ask the Executive Officer if you want to know why."

Zuzu sat back in the cockpit, pondering the answer, when she got word from the bridge: "Entering the atmosphere. Secure yourself and standby to launch."

5 THE TAKING OF GABRIELA ROBIN

Gabriela lead her fellow players through several songs telling the story of the old Martian princess when, at the point where Gabriela sang of the betrayal of the princess by her ambitious cousin, the alarms sounded, and the lighting shifted to combat mode. Stunned, Gabriela looked over at Duke Ireton, who stood and said, "We shall complete this another time!"

Ramsey stood from his chair and looked at the comlink built into his wrist bracer. "They've come, and sooner than expected."

Sibley grabbed Creton and pulled the boy to his side. "What now, my lord?"

"It's Jack." Ramsey said, "And he brought friends."

The Lord Marshall spoke through the castle's speakers: "Secure the ducal family and guests! All men to their stations."

At that moment, explosions erupted around them. Ramsey keyed into the security feed, and he saw more going off at the military spaceport, but fortunately not near *Baden-Powell*.

"Sibley, take Creton and go with the family into the citadel." Ramsey said as he reached for his belt buckle, "I'm certain to be needed outside."

"Spaceport to the castle! Enemy battleship has launched mecha, including an unknown manlike model. Requesting assistance."

Sibley and Ramsey nodded at each other. As Sibley led Creton to catch up with the ducal family and their entourage, Ramsey activated his battle armor. Lines of golden light appeared about him, drawing in the armor about his form. Then the layers within the armor appeared, and the circuitry embedded therein, and finally the pieces became solid locking into place in the process. The donning process completed in the time it took the Iretons and Gabriela to clear the hall.

At this point, only the men-at-arms of House Ireton, Sir Thomas the Lord Marshall, and the household guard remained in the hall. Ramsey caught sight of a cloak dart around a doorway heading out to the spaceport.

"Lord Roland, what are you to do?" Sir Thomas said as Roland headed that same direction.

"I'm going to greet our unannounced guests." Roland said, and out the Grand Hall he went.

A man approached Sir Thomas. "My lord, your orders?"

Sir Thomas sighed and crossed himself. "By God's mercy, we have Lord Roland here to give us a chance to save our Duke and ourselves."

The man looked at Gibson, worried that his master had lost his place in things.

"Reinforce the approach to the family quarters. That's where the attack upon the castle will come."

"And our men outside?

"They are doing their duty for God, Duke, and the Dire March so we can do ours. If you want to help them now, pray to Saint Itano and Saint Hayha for intercession."

The old knight turned about and waved for the men to fall in behind him. "If they want the greatest treasure in all Christendom, then let them come. Let us see if they have the stomach to pay the price in blood and iron to take it from us."

* * *

Ramsey ran out of the Grand Hall, down a corridor and out into a pathway that lead to a stairway up the curtain wall. He paused to see the Ireton Gallowglass mecha struggling against the unknown mecha that launched from Dashing Jack's battleship clearing the skies of Ireton fighters and holding descending cruisers at bay with its guns and missiles. Sweeping across the spaceport below was the tall manlike model, moving with aplomb among the buildings on the surface. It looks like a statue in the image of an armored warrior of antiquity.

Ramsey backed up a space, drew a baton from its boot sheathe, then turned about and ran for the wall's edge. He jumped over the edge, took the baton in both hands, and bellowed "Roland, *draw your sword!*"

The baton separated in the middle, as if held together by magnetism. Ramsey held each half as if it were a joystick controller. From those halves golden lights appeared and drew into place about him a giant-sized armored frame. Then each core subsystem in turn drew into place, followed by the cockpit interior, and finally the lights filled the frame-drawing in.

It became a solid manlike mecha, shaped as a living suit of full plate armor, gleaming royal blue and trimmed in gold, bearing the crest of Roland on its chest, and standing 12 meters tall. The cockpit within lit up, giving Ramsey a 360-degree view about him as the unit's legs kicked forward to fire the thrusters in its feet while the thrusters in its back synched to fire with them. Ramsey landed with a resounding thud, but he landed on both feet and ready for action.

"Behold!" Ramsey yelled, "*Durendal* has arrived!"

The Gallowglass units within range of his voice, boosted by the speakers in Durendal's head, took heart at Ramsey's appearance. "We're saved!" one pilot said, "The Solar Guard stands with us!"

Zuzu cracked a toothy grin within the cockpit of *Anakim*. "There you are!" she said, and she turned *Anakim* to face Ramsey. "I can stop playing with these fools now."

Ramsey looked on as he saw *Anakim* level a long rifle at him. Reading the mech's movements as if he would a living man, Ramsey ran into an empty mecha hangar just as Zuzu fired upon him. He quickly shifted direction once he passed the hangar doors, ducking out of sight, as the follow-up shots drew closer and closer to him.

As he drew his battle rifle, Ramsey noticed the lack of ordinance meant to flush him out of the hangar. He lurched forward and rolled away from the corner he took, taking a hunch as to his enemy's intention, and when he saw the long rifle's barrel break through the wall, he got *Durendal* to its feet and returned fire. Then he aimed up and fired through the hangar roof, where he heard something explode.

"Got one of the smaller ones, my lord!" a Gallowglass pilot said, "But their leader's moving to flank you again."

"My thanks" Ramsey said, intuiting where Zuzu moved and firing another shot that way.

Zuzu hustled around the hangar, trying to out-think her target, only to find him shooting at her from within the hangar as she brought the long rifle up to fire. She reflexively put the rifle in the way, blasting it in half. She discarded the ruined rifle, tossing it aside, in the few moments she had before it exploded and unintentionally destroyed the spaceport's barracks.

More beam rifle rifle came from within the hangar, blowing holes in the wall and forcing Zuzu to dodge. She found a half-wrecked truck, dashed behind him as Ramsey blind-fired at her, picked up the flaming wreckage and then ran for the hangar.

"We bring the pain to you!" Zuzu cried as she crashed through the wall. Ramsey shifted *Durendal's* feet, stepping out of the line of attack, and fired upon the wreckage. The shot blew a hole through what substance remained, making the rest fall apart in *Anakim's* hands. Ramsey fired again, but Zuzu dodged it and pulled a lance from *Anakim's* back. The end ignited, and Ramsey jumped away through the roof to get clear as Zuzu went on the attack. As he descended, he put the rifle away.

She's going to charge, Ramsey thought.

Zuzu did not disappoint. Ramsey drew his beam sword and met Zuzu's charge with a forceful parry. He spun to one side, off the lance's line, and tried to get inside Zuzu's reach. She did not allow it. She mirrored the spin, aiming to catch Ramsey open. She saw an opening, and she delivered a kick that sent Ramsey spiraling through another building as he hurried to reclaim his balance.

Out of the corner of his eyes, he caught Zuzu launching *Anakim* into the air to attempt a Death From Above attack with her beam lance. He got *Durendal*'s feet right and launched into the attack, coming just off her line sweeping up with his beam sword.

Zuzu tried to correct her descent but didn't have enough time. All she could do was watch as Ramsey scored *Anakim*'s breastplate with the tip of his beam sword and then cut her lance in half- but better that then loose an arm or get sliced lengthwise through her cockpit.

Now having reversed the attack, Ramsey turned to descend upon Zuzu, only to find her already moving out of the way and igniting a beam sword of her own.

"Zuzu, stop playing with him!" Gori said as he appeared in a window on her viewscreen, "Back up Jack at the castle."

At the same time, Ramsey saw Sibley pop up in a side window. "My lord, Jack's here with us! We need your arm!"

"Roland to Ireton militia. Report!"

"We're holding here, my lord. The enemy's air support thins, and our ships are coming to our aide."

Ramsey now fixed his eyes upon *Anakim*. "I see what your game is."

Then Ramsey saw Zuzu break off and go to the castle.

* * *

"Here, men." Sir Thomas said, "We stand here."

The old knight stopped before the doors to the ducal family chambers, now sealed, and directed his men to take up positions on either side of the doors. As they did, Thomas got a call over his comlink.

"Lord Marshall, enemy marines descend from the enemy's battleship upon the castle. They're making their move now."

"You know what to do, soldier." Thomas said, "God be with you."

"Yes, my lord." The comlink went silent, and moments later blaster fire and explosions echoed up the hallway from elsewhere in the castle. The men about him checked their rifles, their grenades, and their armor before the sounds of battle began to get close enough to put eyes down the hall. They leveled their rifles, and Gibson drew his pistol.

"We must hold here for as long as we can, men." Thomas said, "Every minute we keep them from the doors is a minute Lord Roland gains to come to our aide."

"For Duke Ireton!" one said.

"That's the spirit", Thomas said, "For God and Duke Ireton!"

"For the Duke!" the rest said in a chorus.

A moment later, Thomas spotted the pirates turning into the hallway. "Here they come! Open fire!"

The Ireton men laid down a stream of red-white hot plasma death down the corridor. The first few pirates to make the turn got caught out, each taking several hits square to the chest and one went down with a hit to the face. But as they slumped like sacks of wheat to the floor their fellows followed up, now sliding across the floor to the far side to get under cover.

"Grenades ready" Thomas said, and a man on either side under cover took up a ball-sized explosive designed for throwing. The pirates now fired back upon them, suppressing more than seeking kills, pushing forward in a classic leapfrog advance tactic up the corridor. First on the left, then the right, and back left the pirates moved so they too could get close enough for ordinance to finish the job.

"Loose!" Gibson said, and the men peaked out to toss their payloads. First one side, then the other, they blew apart the pirates therein and pushed back their advance but more came behind them. The grenadiers immediately ducked back behind cover and took up another grenade, waiting for Gibson's command, as the pirates once more moved up the corridor.

Then the men's rifles ran dry, forcing them to duck and reload, which gave the pirates a chance to close the gap.

"Loose!'

The grenadiers threw their payloads once more, but this time the pirates attempted to shoot both down before reaching their line. One they got, exploding halfway between the two lines, but the other got through and once more forced the pirates back as it detonated and destroyed the advancing edge. The riflemen now finished reloading, and their renewed rifle fire broke the advance entirely. The pirates now scurried back under cover once more.

"We can do this thrice more, my lord. Then we're out" a man said.

"Rifles?"

"Another five magazines apiece, my lord."

Pirate blaster fire increasingly pock-marked the doors to the ducal chambers, but they held. The cycle continued until they ran out of grenades. After that, Thomas successfully feinted a further volley, catching the pirates out one more time, but after that the advance seemed inexorable as they creeped closer and closer to close combat range.

And then one pirate in the back slumped to the floor. Additional blaster fire from down the corridor now penned the pirates in. Caught in a pincer, the pirates soon found themselves cut down to a man. The last one ran back the way he came, hoping to break through and run to regroup with other pirates, only to get impaled upon a beam sword.

The beam winked out, and Thomas now saw plainly who came to their rescue: Count Qis, Sir Lee, and Lee's man Samson.

"Where have you been?" Thomas said as the two men came close, "You should be inside with the duke!"

Lee looked over to Qis, "Samson and I had been seeking my lord the Count here, as he'd been separated from the ducal party in the chaos of the initial assault."

Thomas took a moment to see the logic, but then caught up. "Ah, I see. I can admit you."

Thomas turned around, getting something out from underneath his shirt. "As per house tradition-"

Qis ran Thomas through with his beam sword. "Only the duke and the Lord Marshall have this key."

Before the men could reaction, Sir Lee and Samson cut them all down in a series of sweeping strikes from their own beam swords. "The way is clear, my master."

"You have done well, Sir Lee. Now, to guarantee that none suspect you." Qis said, and he ran Sir Lee through with a second--concealed--sword. Lee looked on, shocked. "Why?" Qis said to the dying man, "Simple. You are no longer useful, and I do not retain liabilities."

Lee joined Thomas and the Ireton men on the floor, and Qis took the pirate insignia Lee had on his person from him. "You died defending your duke, Lee, and only God and I know otherwise."

Qis took the key from Thomas, careful to remove it and the chain it is attached to from about the man's neck. Before opening the doors, Qis took a moment to key into his comlink, listening only.

"I've driven off their ace." Qis heard Ramsey say, "On my way to your side, Sibley."

Qis looked at Samson. "You have a choice. Either you die right here and now, or you enter my service. I have use of you."

Samson kneeled before Qis. "I am your loyal servant."

"Then go to the spaceport and await me by my ship. Your life here is over."

Qis put the key back on Thomas and the insignia back on Lee, in addition to Jack's recording taken earlier. A plan to ensure Jack's success now came to Qis, in case Jack needed it, and back down the corridor he went. No, not to get more pirates, but to accompany Ramsey into a trap that Qis felt certain Ramsey would never see coming. He smirked for a moment, self-satisfied.

* * *

The Duke and Duchess Ireton, followed by Countess Gabriela Robin and her fellow players, entered the family chambers wing of the castle. After the last of their attendants and guards followed, the doors to the wing closed and sealed shut.

"Sir Lee isn't present", Duchess Ireton said.

"He's able to handle himself", Duke Ireton said, keeping his wife's hand in his own, "No doubt he's gone to find our guest's guardian. With Thomas on duty, I have no doubt they will join us in due course. Until then, we are secure here."

A door opened. "No, Your Grace. You are not."

Out into the hallway stepped Dashing Jack. Now he wore the black-and-red attire of the Red Eyes pirates, red-eyed skull insignia on his breast and the brow of the half-mask he wore to cover his eyes, with a pistol in one hand and a beam sword in the other.

"I would prefer that the countess come quietly", Jack said as the ducal party swiftly rearranged itself, putting the guards forth and the men after them while the ladies fled down to the duke's private chambers, "but we must be prepared to deal with disappointment."

"We are a dozen, pirate", Ireton said as he drew his own sword, "A dozen to your one."

Jack looked at them, the red lenses now showing body language analysis of each of them. "You are soon to be several corpses, and several more cripples."

"Take him!" Ireton said, and the guards ignited their blades. Jack shot one down right away with his pistol, and that broke their cohesion. The gap left allowed Jack to get in among them at speed, and he shot a second one dead a heartbeat later. He locked up three more with his beam sword, dooming them to death-by-blaster in turn. The last he feinted with his pistol, stepped inside the guard's reach and ran him through.

Duke Ireton, Sir Conte, and Sibley now came at Jack. Jack saw Sibley draw his pistol, whereas neither Ireton nor Conte had one, so he marked Sibley as the real threat of the three. "Now, Your Grace, I shall do the next part of what I boasted that I would do." Jack said as he blocked Ireton and then Conte while he maneuvered to keep Sibley off his line.

"We are still three to your one", Ireton said.

"An old man, a dandy, and a man-at-arms", Jack laughed, "No, Your Grace. You are two quintains and a fighter against me."

Conte came in at Jack with a chop at his sword arm, but Jack stepped to one side, beat it away and stabbed Conte in the thigh. Ireton followed up, but Jack stepped into the attack and let the duke overshoot. With the duke now off-balance, Jack shoved old Ireton into a wall. Now Sibley shot at Jack, coming in himself, forcing Jack to back away from Conte and instead sweep away Sibley's blow.

As Jack and Sibley faced off, Conte limped over to Ireton and helped the old man to his feet. They took up their swords again, but Conte could barely stand up and Ireton had the wind knocked out of him. Jack and Sibley circled each other, teasing with their swords, seeking an opening. Sibley saw Conte and Ireton and gave them a look.

They came at Jack when the pirate's sword arm was on their side, and Jack countered by sweeping his sword up to parry and push their beam blades away. Sibley fired, hitting Jack along his ribcage, making the pirate cry out from the burning pain, but it was Ireton and Conte that felt the pirate's wrath. He clubbed Ireton with the butt of his pistol square on the bridge of the old man's nose, then pushed him into Conte to bowl both men over.

Sibley fired again, but this time Jack only felt a singe as it scored his shoulder. Jack blindly fired back, but by intuiting Sibley's position Jack forced the graying man-at-arms to move out of the way for a critical moment. As Sibley got back his position, Jack shot both men with his pistol. Their beam swords extinguished as they slumped into the floor, and Jack turned about to face Sibley now.

"Murderer." Sibley said.

"Not so, Sergeant", Jack said, batting it away as if an attack of its own, "They're just out of this fight now, exactly as I said they would."

Sibley and Jack once more began to circle each other. "I'd fought your man before", Sibley said, "I wondered if you trained him."

"Gori needed little instruction." Jack said, "Just how to handle the weapons, and deal with items not build for men of his stature. As for you, I hear that you trained your master."

"In part, but I earned these graying hairs. That's more than I can say for you."

"You think you can hold me until your master comes, don't you?" Jack said, and the lenses of his visor now fed him information of Sibley's past wounds as well as past exploits, "A logical plan, but a futile one."

"True. I don't have to win. I just have to hold you here until my lord arrives."

"You shall be disappointed, Sergeant", Jack said, and he fired. Sibley stepped to one side and shot back before stepping forward. Jack mirrored Sibley's movements, anticipating the graying warrior's sword strike to follow. Sibley did, and Jack locked up Sibley's arm in his parry. He stepped into Sibley's reach, going nose to nose, with both men trying to simultaneously keep from allowing a clear shot to go off.

Several such shots flew in vain as they struggled to break the clench, but when Sibley attempted to wrench his blade free Jack saw it coming. Being the younger man, Jack moved faster and stopped Sibley with a headbutt landing right on the older man's brow.

Wearing the mask, Jack felt nothing and instead drew blood on Sibley. He now broke the clench and fired several times into the man with contact shots into Sibley's barreled chest before running the man through with his sword. Jack kicked away both sword and pistol as the man fell, but he was true to his word and left Sibley alive. He turned to chase after his prize when he saw a boy with a sword in each hand standing in his way.

"Get away from my father!"

Sibley, barely conscious, looked on with a mixture of pride and terror as he saw what Creton, in his boyish manner, had done. Too weak to talk, he could only mouth what he wished to say: "No, boy, no!"

"Brave, boy. Foolish, but brave."

Creton could not stop the rush of emotion come over him and he charged Jack. Jack put his pistol away, and he let Creton flail at him with both blades. He easily met each stroke, without effort batting each back.

"I see that you've had some very basic training. I expect as much from a boy in your position."

"You're not getting away!"

"And I see that you've listened to your father. Good, good." Jack said with a mocking smile, amused.

Creton now executed a feint. A crude, well-telegraphed feint, but a feint nonetheless. Jack let loose a chuckle. "That's a good try, boy!'

Creton came at Jack again, but this time Jack slipped past Creton's guard and destroyed the beam sword in the boy's off-hand. "I refuse to kill you, boy. I refuse to so much as maim you."

Creton paused, put both hands on his one remaining sword, and went back on his guard.

"I won't kill you because of your father, or your master." Jack said, now advancing on the boy and dropping the smile, "I won't kill you because of your display of courage. I won't kill you because of any notion of honor either."

"Then why?"

Jack lunged in, ripped the beam sword out of Creton's hands and tossed it aside. "Because you are nothing, boy! You are not a threat to me!" Jack said as he punched Creton in the guts, making the boy fold over as the wind left him, "And I don't kill what holds no threat to me. I just toss it out with the rest of the trash."

Jack put away his sword, picked up Creton with both arms, wound himself up as if making a hammer throw, and threw Creton out a nearby window. In that moment, he saw a flash of brown as he heard a mecha duel pass by that very window. As he turned back to the scene inside, he laughed.

"Oh my!" Jack said, "It looks like Gori's distaff cousin kept your hero busy all this time!"

In his mask, he heard the following exchange.

"Dammit! Something from inside the castle hit me." Zuzu said into Jack's ear.

"What about it?" Gori said.

"It gave Roland the moment he needed. *Anakim*'s critically damaged. I have to withdraw."

And Jack stopped laughing. Instead, he broke in: "Prize is secured. Gori get ready to pick up. Withdraw Zuzu; I'll activate the backup."

"What about Roland? He's clear to come after you now."

"He has to land, dismount, and make his way here. He's not desperate enough to blast a hole in the roof. Issue the standby orders for withdrawal and departure."

"Aye, Captain."

Jack turned upon the ladies down the hall and calmly stalked towards them, knowing that now nothing could stop him.

* * *

Ramsey moved *Durendal* to pursue Zuzu in *Anakim* back towards the castle. Zuzu picked up a rifle from a destroyed Gallowglass as she ran across the spaceport, and then leaped into the air to clear the outer wall.

Ramsey swapped his beam sword for his rifle again, but instead of a straightforward pursuit he picked up the head from that destroyed unit and carried it with him to the outer wall. He tossed it into the air, and as expected Zuzu fired upon it. This allowed Ramsey to hurdle the wall and fire upon Zuzu, catching *Anakim* twice with hits to its head and shoulder before Zuzu rolled out of the way.

Zuzu glanced over *Anakim*'s system readout, only to see that the headshot left no real damage. The helmet-styling to *Anakim*'s design turned out to be some sort of ablative armor. Ramsey would confirm this, as he now saw *Anakim*'s head clearly. The same applied to the damaged shoulder, as now it too lay exposed. Both Zuzu and Ramsey now understood a critical element of *Anakim*'s design.

"I haven't seen that in some time." Ramsey said over the speakers, "Curious decision."

Zuzu answered by exhausting the rifle's magazine. Ramsey moved as Zuzu brought it up to fire, lifting just off the ground and moving aside with aplomb as he made *Durendal* hover. She threw the rifle at him, and as Ramsey expected she charged at him with Anakim's beam sword. Deftly moving out of the way, Ramsey fired again; he blew off more of the ablative armor on *Anakim*'s frame.

Zuzu lost her cool, now without means to engage at range, and kept attempting to move back into melee with him. Ramsey smiled, sensing that he'd gained the upper hand, and kept his distance. He fired until he depleted his magazine, but by then he'd blown off *Anakim*'s armor entirely. Now he to switch to his beam sword, and at last met Zuzu in melee. He read from *Anakim*'s movements that Zuzu had lost control of herself, and knew it was a matter of time before she would leave an opening that Ramsey could exploit.

It came when they passed by a window in the ducal living quarters. First *Durendal* and then *Anakim* passed, circling each other, when something burst through it and hit *Anakim* from behind as Anakim had its back to the window. Zuzu hesitated, and Ramsey did not; if not for *Anakim*'s sensors systems, Ramsey's thrust would have struck home. Instead, Zuzu saw it just in time and moved the cockpit out of the way. Instead Ramsey skewered through a shoulder between the arm joint and the neck.

"I have you now!" Ramsey bellowed as he reared back to finish Zuzu off.

"Not today!" Zuzu cried as she kicked in the thrusters and shot straight into the air.

Ramsey, remembering the mission, let Zuzu go. She took the damaged Anakim back into the air, where she flew into Revenge's hangar.

* * *

Gori, on the bridge of *Redalen's Revenge*, showed a mask of grim determination as the viewscreen showed yet more Ireton vessels emerging in orbit.

"Send the recall order to the Hobgoblins. We're moving to conclude this operation."

"Aye, Captain." The Communications Officer relayed the order as the turrets fired upon and sunk yet another descending cruiser.

"Captain," Helm said, "we're running out of time!"

"Hobgoblins withdrawing, Captain." Sensors said.

Zuzu broke in over the comlink. "Dammit! Something from inside the castle hit me."

"What about it?" Gori said.

"It gave Roland the moment he needed. *Anakim*'s critically damaged. I have to withdraw."

Gori slammed a fist on the empty captain's chair. "Bridge to Hangar Bay."

"Hangar Bay here. Go ahead."

"The Vice Admiral's withdrawing. Prepare for the captain's unit to sortie and keep a launch path clear as you perform retrievals."

"Aye-aye, Captain! Will do."

Gori now looked at a report of the overall raid. "Comms, get me *Great Gommorah*."

Moments later, *Great Gomorrah*'s captain appeared on screen.

Gori reported, "We're moving to seize the prize now. Get ready to cover our escape."

"Understood, Revenge. Orbital engagement has reached its operational limits. Ireton squadrons from elsewhere are on approach. It's now or never."

"It's now!" Gori said, "Move in to support, and prepare for a speedy retrieval of your Goblins. Your escorts have to hold until you're away."

"That's not going to be easy, Gori."

"At least we have no Solar Guard vessels at our necks."

Now Gori's helmsman spoke up. "We're approaching the target."

"Prepare boarding party."

"Good luck, *Gomorrah*. We'll see you back at base." Gori said to the captain of *Great Gomorrah* as he saluted.

The Captain returned it. "Victory for Babylon!" he said, and the link cut off.

"Hangar to Bridge. We've retrieved the surviving Hobgoblins and the Vice Admiral. *Black Knight* is now launching."

Gori heard a faint cry of excitement, and he knew it came from Zuzu.

"What's with her?" Gori said.

A moment or so later, he got an answer. Zuzu appeared on the comlink, and she hefted a bloodied boy into the viewframe. "We got ourselves a bonus!"

Gori took a moment before he recognized the boy. "Explain how you got Roland's page later. Get both of you to the Infirmary, now."

Zuzu almost objected, and then she remembered who *Revenge*'s captain was. "On our way." she said, dejected.

"Helm", Gori said, "prepare to effect escape once the captain secures the prize."

"Captain," the Weapons Officer said, "we've got enough missiles for one more volley. Shields are close to breaking. We're at our limit."

"Bridge to Engine Room."

"Go ahead, Bridge."

"Are we ready to run?"

"If we can get going in the next few minutes, yes. If we start taking big hits, no."

"Understood."

Now Gori hit a private link to Dashing Jack. "We're in position, we're at our limit, and you need to move!"

* * *

Jack stalked towards Countess Gabriela with deliberate menace, beam sword ignited in one hand and pistol in the other.

"Villain!" Duchess Ireton said, disgusted, "Cad!"

"You are better off running to your husband's side than yelling at me, especially if you wish to see him survive this day." Jack said, "I won't stop you."

Gabriela moved to the Duchess's side. "Go to His Grace." she said, "Your sons are coming. Don't leave them without both of you."

The aging Duchess Ireton clenched her fists, then let loose a sigh. She slowly maneuvered around Jack, and then once past him she hurried back down the hallway to look after her lord and husband.

Now Gabriela went to Lady Maya and took up one of her hands. "Please, be brave for Conte," Gabriela said, and now she took Olga by the hand, "both of you."

Jack waived at them. "Of course. Just get out of the way, and I shall allow you both to save your dandy friend."

They too circled around Jack and then hurried away, pulling Conte apart from old Ireton.

"It is unfortunate that there is no lady for Roland's man, but I doubt he's in any mortal danger." Jack said with a smile, now about sword's length from Gabriela.

"And it is I alone you seek."

"Exactly." Jack said, "You are highly desired, my lady, and there is a most noble lord who will grant great boons to my friends and I in return for delivering you to him."

"You sell your sword in addition to looting and plundering the commerce of Christendom. How base a villain are you?"

"Oh ho, the songbird seeks to shame me?" Jack broke into loud cackling, "You do read too many romances! Go on, look at your noble hostess and your friends. Did I spare their lives out of some sense of honor? Of course not! I spared them for the same reason I did away with that brat; they are neither a threat to me, nor an obstacle to my objective. Why waste time on what does not matter?"

"You dress in passionate colors, and yet all I see is greed for glory and fame, however improper."

"So? You remember Ken and the Necromancer just the same, even though one is clearly the great villain of that past age and the other a most improbable savior. Whom is to remember you if you perish now, Lady Songbird?"

"There is no love in your breast, villain. Not for your fellow man, not for the God who created you, and I doubt even for yourself."

Jack got up into Gabreila's face. "What love resides in my breast is no matter of yours, my lady. You had better concern yourself with what love your future lord and husband bears in his breast instead, and with that I shall put an end to this banter. It is time to submit to your fate, my lady, and prepare for your future life as a wife."

* * *

Count Qis stood in an archway bordering an inner courtyard, one close to the ducal quarters, where he expected Ramsey to put down *Durendal* before running in to stop Jack from taking his cousin Gabriela. He monitored both the ducal and pirate comlink traffic, trying to get a sense of where in the mix his plan had gone. Then came the quick series of commands and reports from *Redalen's Revenge, Anakim's* withdrawal, and the arrival of Ireton reinforcements.

"He should come here now." Qis whispered, thinking aloud, "But where is that Star Knight?"

Just then a thought came to him. Moments before, he heard Zuzu complain of an object distracting her. He also heard Jack toss Ramsey's page out a window. Qis put two and two together and realized what Jack, inadvertently, had done in his hubris.

"And he left Roland an opening." Qis said, slamming a fist against the wall, "This is all about to fall apart."

Then another thought came to him, and Qis ran down another hall. Quickly he located a few Ireton men looking for stragglers and survivors.

"Come with me!" Qis said, "Their captain broke into the duke's quarters. If we don't hurry, he'll take the countess!"

The guards fell in behind Count Qis, and back he went to the sealed chamber door where Thomas and Lee remained in repose along with several others. "Cunning!" Qis said, "He took the door and sealed it behind him."

"My lord." a guard said, "How can we follow?"

"I shall beg His Grace's pardon after the battle for this." Qis said, retrieving the second key from Thomas, "But it is good that few know of House Ireton's tradition of sharing access to secure locations like this, just for these occasions."

Qis unsealed the door while the guards moved the bodies to either side. Another called in the security breach. Qis marked this, knowing he had very limited time to handle matters to his satisfaction, as the doors opened.

"You men are to retrieve His Grace and bear him to safety, along with the Duchess and any other wounded. I will do what I can to hold the villain here until help arrives. Do I make myself understood?"

They all nodded. "Yes, my lord." one said, and they followed him into the ducal chambers. There they found first the very figures Qis expected: a wounded Duke, and several others slain or wounded. Duchess Ireton embraced him as he approached.

"Thank God you've come." She said, "But your coming alone-"

"He died for his Duke, Your Grace." Qis said, "Please, let these men bear you all away to safety. I recommend the Armory for now."

She nodded and waved the men over to her husband and the others. Qis saw them lift first old Ireton, then Sir Conte, and then Sibley onto another's back as if they were firemen and hurry away with their charges.

"Thank you, my lord." Lady Maya said, "Go to her now."

She, Olga, and the Duchess fled to catch up to the guards. Once they were away, and Qis saw that no witnesses remained, he moved on to where he knew he would find Jack, Gabriela and, he suspected, Ramsey.

* * *

Ramsey flew *Durendal* to the open window in the ducal quarters wing. He opened the cockpit and leaped out of *Durendal*, through the open window, and into the wing as *Durendal* came to rest right along the wall. He landed, went into a roll, and came back on his feet drawing sword and blaster as he turned to see Jack menacing Gabreila.

"Stand fast, pirate!" Ramsey said, leveling his pistol at Jack.

Jack returned the gesture. "Right on time, Lord Roland. You do not disappoint."

Gabriela felt a surge in her chest, a brightening of her mood at seeing Ramsey in action.

"You know I hold the High Justice, Dashing Jack. You're not escaping this time."

Jack laughed. "Confident, aren't we?"

"Your ship is beleaguered, at its limit, and will soon be sunk by overwhelming numbers of returning Ireton vessels. Your mecha will be swarmed and destroyed. Your marines are already either dead or broken, and your allies in orbit have either broken and ran or got beaten and died. Now you're backed into a corner with nowhere to run, nowhere to hide, and no useful options left to you. There are none open to you that I haven't already taken measures to cut off."

Jack noticed, far down the hall, Count Qis come forth with Ireton men in tow.

"And using the Countess would not avail me because?"

Ramsey put a shot just over his head.

"I see." Jack said with a shrug, "Fortunately, I am confident with the one measure left to me."

Ramsey saw Jack square off against him, and he mirrored Jack's stance. Gabriela now froze in place, held fast with a mixture of fear and excitement at the two men about to come to blows over her, watching the space pirate and the Star Knight circle each other with beam swords ignited and blaster pistols ready. At that moment, she recognized the danger of getting shot accidentally and scrambled behind and under the duke's desk.

"I see that she's taking a liking to you." Jack said, "That makes this all the more amusing."

"Enough talk!" Ramsay said, and he moved first with a lunging feint. Jack stepped aside, beating the blade away, and then forward to prevent Ramsey from taking a follow-up shot. Ramsey shifted to meet Jack's move, and then cut at Jack's sword arm. Jack stepped into the attack, attempting to lock up Ramsey's blade and get off a contact shot to the guts. Ramsey batted away

Jack's pistol hand, causing the pirate's shot to miss and slam into a wall down the hall.

Now face-to-face, the two men struggled in their grapple to overpower the other. Both men's faces now showed the grimace of determination, their arms straining as their feet struggled to hold, but slowly Ramsey's greater stature showed its quality as he began overbearing Dashing Jack.

Jack, sensing that this clench wasn't going his way, did what he had to do; he rolled backwards and kick-flipped Ramsey over his head and into the wall. Ramsey took that hit on his back, making him fall head-first to the floor and fold over.

Not that Jack had much time to exploit the opening. Realizing that Ramsey's armor was far more than a toughened flight suit, Jack scrambled back to his feet and put down fire towards Ramsey. Ramsey, thanking God and St. Michael for his armor's padding, pushed away from the wall just as Jack began shooting at him. He rolled away from Jack's blazing blaster fire until he got behind a chair, which he then used as a shield while he got on his own feet. When he popped up to return fire, that chair had been blasted to ruin, and he found Jack coming down with his sword at his face.

Jack saw it coming in the nick of time but threw himself off-balance to avoid getting gut-shot, and Ramsey exploited this opening by attacking with his sword. Jack blocked the blow but being off-balance meant being battered about like a leaf on the wind, and Ramsey went for it. One swing after the next, Ramsey pressed and pressed Jack back around the room. While Ramsey kept his swings quick, light, and efficient he aimed them at places awkward for Jack to reach. Jack had to reach them or get cut down.

Jack saw Ramsey's aim was to wear him out, fatigue him, and force a lethal error that way. once more what he must do: he shot at the desk where Gabriela hid. Ramsey remember that fact and struck out at Jack's blaster hand to get Jack to stop. That gave Jack enough time to get steady on his feet, but at the cost of his blaster pistol, a cost Jack immediately remedied by returning the stroke.

"It won't be long now, pirate." Ramsey said, "I can tell that you're fatigued."

Jack now saw Count Qis slowly walking their way. "True, it won't be long, but not as you expect."

"What trick do you think you have to save you now?"

Jack saw *Revenge* notify him now in the lenses of his half-mask: "*Black Knight* is now launching."

"My ship yet sails, Lord Roland. So long as it does, I have yet reason to believe in my victory."

Jack saw Qis coming closer, so he maneuvered Ramsey to face away from the hallway.

"I salute you as a fighting man, Lord Roland. I admire your valor, your determination, and you are worthy of your fame and title. But you share a lacking that I cannot overlook, Roland, a lacking in your acumen that will surely lead to your downfall."

Ramsey stood tall and proud as he kept his beam sword pointed at Jack. "Boldly said, pirate, and you're a better fighter than most I encounter by far, so I'll play along. What do I lack?"

"You do not use your fighting wisdom outside of battle, Lord Roland. That is what will be your undoing."

* * *

Great Gommorah, far away from New Edinburgh, awaited in formation with the others of its line. On its bridge, the Captain monitored the situation.

"Send the withdrawal order. Escorts are to cover the Goblins' withdrawal until all wings are clear, and then they are to fall back to cover our withdrawal back to Dara's Folly."

"Aye, Captain", the Communications Officer said. He repeated the order. One by one, the other carriers reported receipt of the order and their hangar bays prepared to receive returning Goblins as well as whatever plunder they could carry away. The escorting corvettes and cruisers reorganized their formation and moved to cover the retreating mecha, which passed by them at flank speed to their carriers.

The Ireton ships converged, slowing only to reorganize their numbers in turn and bring order to a chaotic and costly response, time which the Red Eyes ships used to best advantage to blunt the Ireton edge further. Using concentrated fire, the Red Eyes escorts focused upon damaged Ireton ships and routed their retreat course through swaths of space already filled with wrecks and debris from earlier in the battle.

The Ireton ships pursued but got slowed down by having to constantly adjust their formation to allow disabled ships to fall away from the formation, and that combined with the route of withdrawal allowed the escorts to complete their mission.

Back on *Great Gomorrah*, the Captain looked at the fighting withdrawal and sighed in relief. "Good. They're too wound up to think clearly."

The Executive Officer appeared on deck and walked up to the Captain. "It looks like your estimation won out, sir. We've got about 5000 Goblins returning."

"One in six losses, for a basic design like that, when we have full surprise and make best use of ambush tactics given the quality of our pilots? I am astounded at the result."

"As for the Hobgoblins, Revenge reports 75% losses."

"That's the more surprising result. A single squadron, against a military garrison, in a new design? The High Admiral will order the immediate switchover of the production lines to the Hobgoblin after this battle."

"We lost a third of our escorts in this action, mostly due to getting caught out when Ireton forces emerged from hyperspace. Most of our mecha losses came from similar circumstances. Against the forces on station when we launched the attack, we did very well and lost nothing."

"Surprise and shock rendering the local defense ineffective and easily blunted, nothing more. We can't count on that going forward."

"Speaking of Revenge, aren't we covering their withdrawal?"

The Captain shook his head. "Their captain already planned for having to make their own way back, so they're going with that plan instead. We're fall back to Dara's Folly as soon as possible and regroup there for the final phase of the operation."

The Executive Officer stood there for a moment, scratching his chin. "Captain, what is the final phase of this operation?"

The Captain smiled. "Their utter defeat."

* * *

Jack stepped behind the desk, and with a foot he pushed over. Then he grabbed Gabriela, now revealed, and pulled her to her feet.

"This, Lord Roland, is what shall symbolize your defeat today and your demise tomorrow." Jack said as Gabriela tried to get free of his grip, "You, like her, are too fond of seeing things only as you are long-accustomed and not as they truly are."

Ramsey was not impressed. "Your argument is unconvincing, and neither is your attempt to make a hostage of the Countess. If you had sense, you'd release her and quit this scheme."

Jack saw in his half-mask the distance measuring how far away his Black Knight was now and he smiled. "Quit? Oh, I shall quit this all right, because this battle is over and both you and the Countless will be forced to acknowledge reality presently."

Now Gabriela noticed her cousin, Count Qis coming clearly into view and she let her hope show on her face, a smile Jack also noticed. He turned her about and faced her towards Ramsey and Qis.

"Both of you shall now see that your lingering childish Romanticism has cost you both your victories this day." Jack said, marking that Black Knight had now arrived and was about to be right on the other side of the wall. A faint echo of a descending flyer came into the room from the hallway just beyond, but neither Ramsey nor Gabriela had any notion of what that meant.

In Jack's ears, he heard Gori say: "We're in position, we're at our limit, and you need to move!"

Jack pushed Gabriela forward, following along and binding her arm behind her to keep her controlled. Then a bright red-white beam going from floor to ceiling swept away the wall behind Jack. The rear wall now destroyed, it revealed a black-and-red mecha hovering and closing to press against the opening. It rose just enough to show the cockpit in the torso open, to reveal it had no living pilot within.

"This is your plan to escape?" Ramsey said, "You think that I can't pursue in *Durendal*? That I won't? That I can't catch you, and pull you out of that cockpit? That I won't rescue Gabriela?"

That use of her Christian name caught not just the notice of Gabriela, but also of Qis and Jack. "Roland, my lord, please don't despair!"

"Despair has no home here." he said, "Soon this will be over."

Now both Gabreila and Jack saw Qis step behind Ramsey, but the noise of Black Knight's engines drowned out the footfalls.

"Indeed, Lord Roland, it is." Jack said, and then Qis shot Ramsey in the back multiple times with his blaster in rapid succession, dropping Ramsey to the floor.

"ROLAND!" Gabriela bellowed, reverberating down the hallways. Then she turned to her cousin, "Why?"

"A man can have anything, if he is willing to sacrifice" Qis said, "To become Emperor of all Christendom, I sacrifice you, Cousin."

* * *

Zuzu the Painbringer stepped on to the deck of *Redalen's Revenge*, where she found Gori staring at the main viewscreen.

"What's our status, Gori?"

"*Black Knight* is at the castle and just cleared an escape route for the Captain." Gori said, and then a window popped up with Dashing Jack's smug face on it.

"Prize secured, Gori."

Both Gori and Zuzu heard the cries of a woman come over the comlink.

"She's in shock." Jack said, "Seeing her Romantic delusions shattered before her eyes proved too much for our songbird to bear. That should be enough to get her aboard ship and in her quarters. Prepare to retrieve."

"Aye, Captain!" Gori said with a toothy grin, "Well done! What about our Solar Guardsman?"

"Down and out, if not dead, thanks to our inside man."

Gori and Zuzu shared a laugh.

"And Zuzu, I would appreciate it if you personally escorted our most noble guest to her quarters."

"I would be honored, Captain." Zuzu felt a wave of satisfaction flow through her, "And I prepared a plaything to keep her occupied."

"Oh?"

"Roland's page boy somehow fell into my arms, so he'll be waiting for our guest when she arrives."

Jack immediately connected cause to effect and laughed at his good fortune. "Did you hear that?" Jack said, looking off-screen, "You get to look after Roland's little boy! It's almost like having a doll or a puppy to play with!"

Gori and Zuzu saw a fist futilely hit Jack's half-mask in protest.

Gori turned to the Helmsman who said, "*Black Knight* is on approach, and we're in position to cover retrieval."

"Prepare to move to flank speed along the escape route as soon as the Captain's mecha is secure. Don't even wait for the ramp to close. Once we begin our ascent through the atmosphere, spin up the hyperdrive. I want to jump to Dara's Folly as soon as we're clear."

"Aye-aye, Captain."

Then Gori turned to the Weapons Officer. "Fire our final volley of missiles at that point. We won't stay in range of their guns for long after that, and once we've shaken this lot we're as good as gone."

Moments later, Jack said: "The Countess and I are aboard. Get us out of here, Gori!"

"You heard the Captain, move!"

Revenge launched her final missiles as the engines moved to flank speed, breaking away from the pursing Ireton cruisers and corvettes coming after her. Her guns finished the vessels that the missiles hit, and then drove off the rest. She ascended to altitude and flew around to where the orbital fleets had again left a void In their reach. At that point she began a hard ascent up through the atmosphere, moving at speed while spinning up its hyperdrive. The clouds thinned, the ship moved into space, and as soon as they got clear of New Edinburgh's orbital sphere Dashing Jack gave the command.

"Punch it!"

* * *

"Make way for the Duke." Sibley heard, and he struggled to rise to his feet. A nurse helped him stand steady as Duke Ireton got wheeled into the room.

"God's truth, Sibley, I am pleased to see you alive." Duke Ireton said, "I'd been coming to see everyone here. What say the doctors?"

"So long as he or I are in our battle armor, anything short of instant death can be survived, Your Grace." Sibley said, "Once the armor completes its auto-repair, it will immediately begin healing the wearer."

"And Lord Roland?"

"The stroke struck several vital organs. He will be unconscious for many hours yet. Have your men recovered the items I asked for?"

Duke Ireton waved a boy forward. "We found this baton outside the window, as you suspected. The rest came with Lord Roland."

Sibley pointed to the table next to his bed. "I'll take these to *Baden-Powell* as soon as I'm able. Is there still no sign of my son?"

Duchess Ireton now came into the room. "No, good Sergeant."

Now Count Qis came into the room. "Ah, good. I'd been meaning to find both of you."

"I'm told that it is you that opened the barred door." Duke Ireton said, looking the count over, "We shall speak of that issue later. For now, my thanks in seeing to our safety in place of Sir Thomas."

"And in revealing the treachery of Sir Lee." Duchess Ireton said, "I still can't believe he turned his coat against us. After all these years, and to think we knew not the depths of his bitterness."

"We can be certain he is responsible for our noble lord's near-death also." Qis said, "By your leave, Your Grace, I shall consult with my family on this matter."

Duke Ireton nodded, and Qis left. "I'll be back later, Sibley, to see about Roland."

Then he and the Duchess left with their attendants, and then the nurse. Once gone, Sibley closed the door and keyed into a tablet. A moment later he had a secure connection back to Palatine Hill on Earth, and an old man bearing the livery of Archangel Michael appeared on the screen.

"Still alive, Sibley!" Duke Michael said.

"Yes, Your Grace. You know why I call, I suspect."

"Bad news travels fast, old friend. Did you break my boy?"

"He's being put back together as we speak, and I'm monitoring his progress just in case. Do you think this warrants an acceleration procedure?"

"Maybe. I take it Ireton's still hot-headed in his old age?"

"Not as he was in his youth, but his sons are more than akin to their father to make up for it. They already sailed to pursue the pirates back to the asteroid belt they came out of."

"You think it's a trap?"

"Certainly. To what end remains to determined."

"And you think that the outcome of that battle will enough to authorize the use of restricted measures?"

"Your Grace, compare the new ace model to those grunt models and tell me the angel we've been hunting isn't present."

"All right, Sibley. If they demonstrate a serious threat, I will authorize it. Let's hope they're not anticipating us intervening like this."

6 IRETON'S COUNTERATTACK

Duke Ireton sat in the Armory of Scarborough Castle in a wheelchair overseeing the gathering of House naval assets when an alert notified him of a massive hammerhead-shaped battleship emerging from hyperspace.

"*Prince Charles* to Scarborough Castle", said an Ireton scion, appeared as a 3d hologram over a war planning table.

"Scarborough Castle here", Ireton said. "Welcome home, son."

"Rear Admiral Count Joshua Ireton, reporting in", the scion said. "Praise be to God that you are alive, Father."

"Your brothers and cousins are getting impatient," Ireton said, "I'm counting upon you to do what I cannot."

"Are we alone on this?"

"Count Qis speaks to his friends and family, as has your mother on our behalf, but only the Solar Guard stands any chance of coming to our aide for now."

Joshua nodded. "Speaking of the Guard, what of Lord Roland?"

"Out of danger, but still in the Infirmary", Ireton said. "The security records are corrupted, but we do know that someone shot him square in the back while Dashing Jack held his full attention. We suspect that Sir Lee did that deed also, but we cannot confirm that."

"I've reviewed the after-action reports filed so far. I think we can handle this on our own, but it will require a serious attitude. Being dismissive is how we got into this situation, Father."

"Agreed, and I have said as much to your brothers and cousins. The muster should be complete presently, so you have little time to wait before departing for Dara's Folly."

"Who remains to arrive?"

"Your cousin Geoffrey, coming in *Wallace*, and your brother Samuel in *Bruce*."

50

An aide leaned in and whispered to Ireton ear. "Son, I'm needed elsewhere. You have your orders. Good luck, and for your mother's sake come home alive."

"Tell Mother to pray to St. Itano then", Joshua said. "*Prince Charles*, over and out."

As the viewscreen returned to the view of orbital space, Count Joshua turned to his Executive officer. "Fortunately, I don't need to worry about my uncles this time. It will be hard enough maintaining discipline as it is."

"Only one battleship, my lord?" the Executive Officer said. "Are you certain we can afford to dispatch without another?"

"Their forces came with only one, had the element of surprise, and withdrew as soon as we arrived in force. I think we can handle them even if they have a position they can fight from, especially now that His Grace authorized the use of the munitions I requested."

The Executive Officer looked at a manifest of the munitions to be transferred to Prince Charles. "Antimatter warheads, my lord?"

"I told His Grace years ago that Dara's Folly should have been cleaned out, and now comes the opportunity to do so. I'm taking it, and I won't be denied this time. Whatever scheme they intend, it requires space to use effectively, space I will deny them by using these warheads."

* * *

Redalen's Revenge pulled alongside *Great Gomorrah*. Hangar bays opened, and *Anakim* transferred from the battleship to the carrier along with its pilot. As the bays closed up, one voice spoke: "Vice Admiral Zuzu, in *Anakim*, returning."

In *Great Gomorrah*'s hangar bay, the men ceased what they did and saluted their mistress. She returned their salute curtly as she hurried to the bridge, where she saw the ship's captain on duty in his chair monitoring Dara's Folly and the whole of the fleet's action about them.

"Admiral on deck." The bridge crew took a moment to stand and salute their mistress now.

"As you were", Zuzu said. "Captain, report."

"Combat losses were within expectations, Admiral." he said, "A thousand Goblins lost in action, all but a few due to combat. The rest were within the expected rate of mechanical failure. The pilots followed procedure and self-destructed. None survived thereafter to be recovered."

"Ship strength?"

"Every escort took hits, but none are too damaged to remain. We have repairs being rushed across the fleet now, following procedure. The carriers need to replenish their ordinance but are otherwise undamaged. You would know first-hand what condition *Revenge* is in."

"I saw a courier in the bay. What of that?"

The Captain smiled. "Your eyes only, straight from the High Admiral."

"I'll be in my quarters. Route any calls to me there for now."

"Very good, Vice Admiral." the Captain said, and Zuzu hurried to her quarters. Once alone, she opened the box and took the mini-disk therein and slotted it into a portable holo-imager. A 3d recording of her brother Red Eyes appeared.

"Sister, I'm presuming that the operation has gone as planned so far, and that you are now at Dara's Folly with our prize in your possession preparing to ambush House Ireton's counterattack. I'm sending you this message now to inform you that you need not worry about the condition of the fleet or how the ambush goes. You will find in this package a key. When you conclude this message, go to your flagship's bridge and have the captain insert this key. You will be required to give authorization by voice, but once finished you will have the secure link back to base necessary to act as a homing beacon."

"Homing beacon? But we have no reserves right now?" Zuzu said, thinking aloud.

"If your ambush threatens to turn against you, call back to base and I shall send forth the guarantee of victory that you shall require, complements of the Chief Architect."

"The Chief Architect? But that must mean-"

"The activation phrase is 'Come Babylon', so be mindful once the beacon is active. You won't have to worry about what to do from there. Just finish the job, and then you can return home in glory."

The super robot is ready to deploy! Zuzu thought, and that thought made her cackle.

* * *

Prince Charles gathered the rest of the Ireton fleet about it, leaving only the assigned garrison ships and mecha behind to begin its pursuit of the Red Eyes fleet towards Dara's Folly. Joshua came on to the bridge and took his chair when he heard alerts coming through.

"My lord Admiral," the ship's captain said, "*Robert the Bruce* and *William Wallace* have arrived and are hailing."

"Main screen, Captain."

Joshua saw his cousin Commodore Sir Geoffrey Sturgeon appear, saluting, and then his brother Commodore Count Samuel Ireton appeared and saluted.

"Reporting for duty", they said in unison. Then they realized both men were on with Joshua at the same time and scowled at each other.

"Commodores." Joshua, "You two will anchor either end of the battle line, following the plan you received previously. I am counting on you two to execute that plan. Our objective is the rescue of the Countess, and everything is secondary to that."

"You're certain that they'll attempt an ambush?" Geoffrey said?

"The Admiral is certain." Samuel said before Joshua could answer, "He and His Grace the Duke conferred before we arrived. If this is the plan, then they are confident that their assessment of the enemy's aims is accurate."

"Enough!" Joshua held forth a hand, "I won't have this banter."

Joshua gave both of his subordinates a stern glare.

"The ordinance issued to your vessels shall arrive presently. I expect that both of you shall receive and store that ordinance with great care. Until I order otherwise, adhere to the plan."

"Yes, my lord Admiral!" they said, and their windows closed. Joshua's Executive Officer stepped forward.

"Concerned, my lord Admiral?"

"Greatly. Our fathers aren't coming out this time, for one reason or another, taking up rear positions and managing garrisons in the event of this being a bigger feint."

"Another?"

"That's the cover story my uncles will use. The reality is that they see this affair as far more manageable than it is. They think that once the hot-heads get their noses broken that they can step forth and negotiate a ransom. They fail to comprehend that these pirates came in heretofore unseen strength, unseen numbers, and unseen sophistication of tactics. They also fail to comprehend the importance of a Star Knight's presence. They don't know when a pirate is an agent of a hostile power, instead of being just star-faring thieves."

"And your noble father?"

"Caught between foot-dragging vassals and a worrisome lord. If this battle succeeds, then it justifies the inaction of Father's vassals. If it fails, then it threatens Father's position."

"And yours."

"And Ireton's posterity thereafter." Joshua said, "I still cannot believe Mother convinced Father to issue that command performance as a means of demonstrating our power and prestige in taming the Dire March. Not when most of the worlds remain clear frontier territory in need of taming. Count Qis' silvered tongue is to blame."

* * *

Aboard *Redalen's Revenge*, Gabriela sat on the bed in her cell euphemistically deemed "quarters", but located in the ship's brig, cradling Creton's head in her lap. A viewscreen in the wall by the door turned on.

"My lady", Jack said, "if you hold out hope that your hosts shall board my ship and break you and your ward from that cell, then I invite you to watch as you see how well we've measured your most noble allies. Even as I speak, we prepare once more to push the odds to our favor."

Gabriela got up, carefully shifting off the bed. "What could you do to me that you have not done?"

"You yet hope for deliverance." Jack said, his face turning to that self-satisfied smirk that began to grate on her, "This is the end of all hope, as you shall soon see."

Gabriela turned away from the screen, putting her eyes on Creton now, checking his bandages.

"Soon, my lady, you too shall see with your own eyes this world as it is. There is a limit to the power of your precious civilization, and out here that limit is not hard to see in action. Once your Ireton friends are crushed, none shall rally further to save you. Fear shall freeze their hearts solid, and frozen hearts risk nothing for no one no matter how acclaimed the object may be."

Gabriela made to move between the screen and Creton, as if discretely looking under the boy's shirt, but really rummaging through his belt and pockets. He must have some emergency transmitter. she thought, Ah, there it is!

She found the transmitter, a stylus-sized item, and slipped it into the sleeve of her dress. "I'm told that you're being sensible about taking meals. I knew putting Roland's boy in your care would provoke you to be sensible, and it will help you practice the habits you will need in your future soon to come."

Gabriela now turned back to the screen. "Creton needs his bandages changed, and with that he should be bathed."

"Of course. I will have an orderly by your quarters before we initiate combat. Take your meal before then, as I must seal that wing once we initiate operations."

"How long?"

"Oh, I estimate a few hours. Enough to ensure we're all rested, fed, and ready for battle."

"Very well then. Soon, Captain."

"Soon." Then the viewscreen shut off.

Jack, sitting in his chair on the bridge, turned to Gori.

"She's going to try to warn them." Gori said.

"Of course. Did you plant the transmitter?"

"As ordered, on the frequency specified."

"Soon we'll see if our heroic knight is with us or not." Jack said, "As for our guest, how crushing will it be for her to realize that she is the one that lured those Ireton fools to their deaths?"

"We shouldn't break her, Captain. That's the groom's job." Gori said.

* * *

An Ireton scout ship approached Dara's Folly. Inside its slim hull, the crew gathered and took up their seats on the bridge."

Captain, all systems are green." the Helmsman said, "No hostiles within sensor range."

"Engage masking. Ready drones." The Captain brought up the mission plan on the main viewscreen. "The first sweep will identify targets for the approach. The second will sweep the rescue approaches to the colony's headquarters. We are to identify and mark hostiles, but not to engage."

"Drones are ready", the operators said.

"We have a link to *Prince Charles*", the Communications Officer said, "so we are ready to go."

"Deploy the drones."

On the outside of the ship's hull, a dozen man-sized units detached and extended their legs. Green lights lit up, and away the dozen drones went into the asteroid belt. They split up into three flights of four, quickly diverging into flight paths going over and under the local plane. The drone operators, each monitoring a flight of four, kept an eye on the live monitors while the Communications Officer ensured that the feeds remained secured coming into the ship and repeating out to *Prince Charles*.

The Captain kept his eyes on the main viewscreen, switching the drone of focus every so often. As the drones finished the first pass, he marked out several asteroids as potential targets for the fleet's attention once they begin the approach. The drone operators also flagged several patrolling Goblins, some lying in wait and some actively on patrol. As the drones began their second pass, many more Goblins got identified and marked.

"Use the vertical infiltration path for the colony's headquarters", the Captain said.

The drone operators came at the headquarters from above and below the plane, pausing to let patrolling Goblins pass, and using personnel airlocks to infiltrate the facility. Once inside, they spread out to seek out the colony's operations center, its powerplant, and its armory: the three most secure parts, and thus the most likely areas for the enemy to put a prize. The drones found an active garrison of pirates, and all three secure rooms locked down. They couldn't even get into any security feeds to see inside remotely.

The Captain switched to a private channel to speak with Count Joshua. "My lord Admiral, everything seems as we expected, but we cannot confirm either the objective or enemy leadership being present."

Count Joshua now appeared in the Captain's private viewscreen. "If they have a carrier capable of running their operations, their leadership may be aboard that ship instead."

"That still leaves a lack of confirmation of the objective, my lord Admiral."

"Captain", one of the drone operations said, "we've gotten into the air ducts. We've got eyes on each of the secured areas. We confirm no leaders present."

"The objective?" the Captain said.

"No eyes, only audio", another operator said.

"Audio? Fine, patch it through."

They heard only faint sobbing, but the voiceprint came back as that of Countess Robin.

"Captain," the Communications Officer said, "we're getting a transmission on an emergency frequency. It's the Countess."

"Put her through."

The main screen showed no video. "Ireton fleet, this is Countess Gabriela Robin. I call to you using an emergency transmitter supplied by Lord Roland's page, who is also imprisoned with me. I call to you with a warning. The pirates intend to ambush you at Dara's Folly. They mean to draw you in, englobe you, and destroy you before you are able to respond and escape."

"Any sign of the page boy?" the Captain said.

"No, Captain, but we can presume that he's unconscious according to the reports. If she's transmitting, then he's with her."

"My lord Admiral?" the Captain said.

"Don't respond." Joshua said, "Trace the signal if you can."

"Communications, trace that transmission."

The moments passed, and tension tightened in the chests of the crew. "It's no good, Captain. The best I can do is say that she's near the center of the belt."

"Captain," Joshua said, "recall your drones and withdraw. File your report on your way back to the fleet. We have enough to proceed."

"Yes, my lord Admiral." Joshua's window closed, and the Captain turned his attention to the crew. "Recall the drones. Helm plot our egress course back to the fleet. We're done here."

The operators slipped their drones back out of the colony headquarters as they came in, and once back in space they issued the recall order and waited for the drones to come out of the belt and reattach to the hull.

"Helm, get ready to run" the Captain said.

"You think they're going to come at us?" the Helmsman said as he turned the ship around.

"If I were one of those pirates", the Captain said, "and I fancied myself a tactical genius, I would presume that the enemy would scout the battlefield before approaching and be on the lookout for scouts. If I found one, I'd follow it back as far as I could manage and then report back where the enemy fleet was. If I couldn't manage to follow, I'd call it in and swarm the scout to prevent their report."

"Captain, begging your pardon sir, but that sounds stupid. Would they not realize that we could report remotely?"

"If they were true geniuses, then they wouldn't be pirates."

"Drones returning", one of the operators said, "and beginning retrieval operations."

One by one, the dozen drones reattached to the hull and powered down. No one noticed that one had a homing beacon attached.

"Retrieval complete, Captain."

"Helm, full speed ahead."

The Ireton scout ship withdrew at best speed.

On *Revenge* Jack and Gori watched as the homing beacon came through clearly.

"Captain, why did you order that beacon planted?"

"Because the High Admiral ordered that it be planted. I got the word from the Painbringer and had to dispatch a courier to the facility to get it done."

"What does he have in mind?"

"Whatever it is, Gori, it made the Vice Admiral giddy."

"The fools are doomed."

* * *

The Ireton fleet closed on Dara's Folly. With *Prince Charles* at the center, the fleet sailed in a double-winged formation for maximum firepower. On either end of the wings were one of the heavy cruisers: *Robert The Bruce* on the left, and *William Wallace* on the right. Combined this came to a force of a thousand capital ships and their escorts.

"All ships", Joshua said, "this is the Admiral. We begin our attack soon. All ships shall prepare their mission ordinance at this time and launch on my command."

Across the fleet, gunnery crews loaded missiles tipped with anti-matter warheads into their launchers. Gunnery officers punched their assigned targets into their computers, and command officers awaited the order to launch.

"My lord Admiral", *Prince Charles'* captain said, "the fleet has reached the 10-thousand-kilometer mark."

"Halt here." Joshua said.

In moments, the entire fleet halted.

With a wave of his hand, Joshua said "Launch!"

The Ireton fleet launched its first volley of anti-matter missiles into the asteroid belt. These missiles went above and below the plane and went far wide of the facility. Aboard *Great Gomorrah* and *Redalen's Revenge,* they looked on at first confused. Then Jack got on the comlink to *Great Gommorah*: "Get the ships away from the belt!"

The warheads detonated simultaneously, obliterating everything around it for several kilometers apiece. Now a wide void on either side of Dara's Folly appeared on the viewscreens of both sides, as if the Ireton fleet had sliced off a length of the belt. The crews quickly reloaded the launchers and the gunners entered in the second set of coordinates.

"Launch!"

The second volley sliced off another section of the belt on either side, shrinking the remaining asteroid presence. The crews reloaded, the gunners changed their targets, and now the Red Eyes ships scrambled to get out of the belt as their buffer to the outside on either side had disappeared. Goblins scrambled out of their hiding spots to retreat towards the facility or back to their carriers.

"Launch!"

The final volley cleared out the asteroids between the fleet and the central facility, catching scores of Goblins and several ships hiding among them in the process. Several more sustained critical damage and had to be abandoned due to being rendered unfit for action. Crews and pilots set their machines to self-destruct and fell back to the facility, taking up defensive positions once within its walls.

"Advance!"

The crews now switched back to conventional warheads as the fleet moved forward once more. As they approached, the formation expanded upward and downward as the wings folded in on either side. Once they reached five thousand kilometers, gunners input another set of coordinates and awaited the order to launch.

Meanwhile Zuzu, on the bridge of *Great Gommorah*, slammed her fists on a railing.

"Get me *Revenge!*"

A moment later, Jack's smug face appeared in a window. "You called, Vice Admiral?"

"They've blown apart most of the belt we need. Now what?"

"Fake a retreat", Jack said. "Take the carriers and fall back as if we're egressing. Take the wings within them with you."

Zuzu nodded her head. "They'll anticipate it."

"We need only keep them thinking they've tricked us until we've boxed them in. Once you're out of contact range, split the carriers and have them move to flank positions. Launch the wings when they've taken the bait and begin boxing them in. We'll make this work yet."

"Agreed." Zuzu said, and she cut Jack off. Turning to the Captain, she said "Take this ship to the rear. All carriers are to follow suit. Cruisers stay with Revenge; everyone else cover our withdrawal."

As the carriers fired up their drives and turned about, *Revenge* moved up and the cruisers formed up around the battleship.

On *Prince Charles*, Count Joshua saw the pirate movements and smiled. "Advance forward, slowly bringing in the wings. Deploy the Gallowglasses and let them clear away hostiles near the facility."

From hangar bays and hull-attached units hundreds of pilots launched and moved into the battlefield. Unit by unit they found and engaged Goblins waiting for them, provoking fierce close combat engagements. The ships slowly chipped away at the Red Eyes capital ships, catching those that slipped into range but out of cover with long-range fire.

"Squeeze them into the center and push the center back until we can gain the facility and clear it."

Jack saw the Ireton fleet's maneuvers and smiled. "Bait in their wings, make them think they've got this. Slowly pull back on my position."

The Red Eyes cruisers rallied, playing their role well. As they pulled back towards *Revenge*, *Revenge* slowly pulled back through the belt to the rear, giving the Ireton fleet the impression of executing a fighting withdrawal while the weaker ships withdraw entirely. The carriers now were on the edge of sensor range for Jack, making them off the Ireton fleet's range entirely.

"Signal Zuzu to split the carriers and advance to the enemy's flanks."

Zuzu gave the order, and the carrier group split in half. Each half skirted the combat zone, taking care to remain out of sensor range, while their Goblin wings prepared to launch and join the fight.

Ireton Gallowglass units reached the facility and secured the docking bay. "Send the landing party. Secure the objective."

A shuttle launched from *Prince Charles* with marines ready to deploy. They passed through the battlefield unmolested and landed in the facility's docking bay. They disembarked, methodically exterminating the pirates within with blaster fire and ordinance. The Ireton ships without, having eliminated resistance without, moved in to secure the space about the facility.

"Signal Zuzu", Jack said. "Launch all mecha. We have the beacon's signal?"
"Confirmed." Gori said.
"All ships are to lock on to that signal and fire until destroyed."

Inside, the marines finished securing the facility.
"She's not here, Admiral."
Klaxons sounded. A hundred missiles from three directions converged on *Prince Charles*.
"We were warned, and we still fell for it!" Joshua said.

* * *

Red Eyes strode into the main dry dock in Hell's Heart. He walked up behind an impossibly handsome man in the prime of his life, whom he saw looking on a massive robot, the length of a cruiser, laying on its back. It was a manlike design, but with a bull's head.

"It's ready, my boy", the man said. "Your sister should not find it difficult to figure out how to use it."

"This is your idea of a simple design?"

"It's a testbed model, as much as that smaller one I sent for your sister to use", the man said. "Most of what is present here is going to be used in future models, but I want to get a practical combat test before making final design decisions."

"You mean that they are not wholly reliable", Red Eyes said.

"The only true test of a combat machine is combat. Your sister is tough. She'll survive if it blows up."

"Does it have a name?"

"Not yet. You want something properly menacing, don't you?" the man said.

Red Eyes nodded.

"These illiterates will call it 'Minotaur', so we'll use that", the man said. "If it survives, we can properly name it something more fitting."

"I will remember that, Artificer."

A misshapen man hobbled up to the two of them. "Master", the cripple said to Red Eyes, "we have a clear signal from the Vice Admiral's position."

"And?" Red Eyes said.

"The operation proceeds within expectations" the cripple said, "but the enemy has attempted to reverse the ambush strategy."

"Has attempted?" Red Eyes said.

"Yes, Master. Captain Jack turned it back and reasserted our intended strategic plan, but the situation remains fluid and could turn against us again."

The Artificer laughed. "I would rather see your sister sweat some and bring this machine out."

"Master", the cripple said, "we also report both a clear signal to the summoning beacon as well as to a homing beacon."

"But they are not in the same exact location?"

"No. One is on the flagship, and the other on the enemy flagship."

"Dismissed. Begone!" Red Eyes said, shooing the cripple away. Then he returned his attention to the Artificer. "My sister didn't come up with this plan. It must be Jack."

"Oh? I recall that you didn't brief him on the robot."

"He would figure it out in time, and it looks like he has. The use of the beacon to easily target their flagship with conventional weapons is his excuse, but I know his cunning; he's aware that when we deploy the robot it will come out at the strongest signal point, and with that beacon in place-"

"-it comes out on top of their flagship. Cunning, indeed. I see why you tolerate him."

"That's not all. Once he sees that the robot has arrived, he will take his ship and withdraw, orders or no orders. If it weren't for the precious cargo in his hands, I would not tolerate desertion in the face of the enemy."

"But he does, so you will."

* * *

"Shoot those missiles down!" Count Joshua bellowed.

The point-defense cannons on *Prince Charles* as well as the escorting frigates and destroyers nearby filled the space with fire aimed at the volley streaming in from beyond. Most of the first volley took hits and went down before reaching the target. Some more took glancing hits that drove the warhead off its course and hit one of the escorts instead. The second volley did better at negotiating the counter-battery fire but ended up hitting more of the smaller vessels near *Prince Charles*.

"Our screen is getting shredded!" Joshua said.

"Thousands of new contacts on both sides, engaging the wings."

On the main screen, the wings from the carriers now came into sensor range and closed fast on the edges of the formation where few large ships were.

Without any mecha to intercept, and anti-mecha fire from the point-defense cannons being limited in effectiveness, the Goblins easily closed to effective range to barrage from the missile pods attached to their torsos.

The point-defense cannons shifted fire to the missile barrages, screening the Goblins behind them as they closed, and now the pirates broke through and fired at close range. Soon the smallest vessels in the formation went down, and once the Goblins got close, they stayed close to complicate counterfire.

"Where are our mecha?" Joshua said.

"Engaged within the belt and around the facility, my lord Admiral." the Captain said.

On the bridge of *Revenge*, Jack laughed as he saw the shift in the situation. "Forward!"

The battleship and the cruisers with it now rejoined the fight, launching their own mecha to clear out Ireton's and engaging the beleaguered Ireton flagship group at long range. Revenge's primary guns alone sunk a single Ireton vessel per turret, per volley of fire.

"Fix them fast. We need only hold them in place." Jack said, and then he turned to Gori, who nodded and sent a signal to Zuzu.

Zuzu took the summoning beacon and left the bridge of *Great Gammorah*, but instead of making for the hangar bay she ascended to a dorsal hull hatch. With nothing more than a sealed suit and a rocket pack she sortied into the fray, flying as a missile for and above Prince Charles.

"Here it comes, Gori", Jack said, monitoring the progress. "This will be the stroke that breaks their backs. They dare not come against us again after this moment."

Count Joshua looked on as his fleet disintegrated on the wings. His mecha got swept from space, and the missiles kept pummeling his fleet's defenses. Enemy mecha ate his wings like locusts, and now the enemy's battleline advanced upon him again blowing apart his escorts with ease.

Now Zuzu had a clear visual sighting of *Prince Charles*. She ascended above the plane of battle, held the summoning beacon and hit the button: "COME, BABYLON!"
With the roar of a bull, a cruiser-sized bull-headed robot appeared overhead of *Prince Charles*, with Zuzu inside. Red eyes lit up in the sockets, and as the cockpit lit up within, showing her that she wore the robot like a suit and could see all about her as if its head were her own. In moments she saw images in her mind telling what to do and how to do it, and she let fly a maniacal cackle.
"Behold the revenge of Babylon!" she said. Within the Ireton fleet all hands heard her taunt: "Fires of Baal, BURN!"
The mount of the robot opened as Zuzu gathered some distance from *Prince Charles*. In the vacuum of space, the attack was a raw beam that struck the Ireton flagship at its bow along the dorsal hull. She swept the beam along its spine, down to the stern, slicing the battleship apart until the beam hit the engines and set them off. The force of the explosion unleashed such a violence of force that it engulfed all within a kilometer around it, save for Minotaur.
Zuzu turned that beam about the nearby ships and sliced them apart. The resulting explosions threw Zuzu into a frenzy of laughter. Engaging the thrusters without thought, she flew forward at the nearest cruiser. She tilted the head down and rammed it, blowing through it with ease.

"*Great Gommorah*," Jack said, "we've finished this job. If they withdraw, let them try. If they get past the Vice Admiral, then they can have their lives."

Now Commodore Sturgeon called upon Commodore Ireton. "What now?"
"I'm taking command", Ireton said. "We're retreating. You take your half. I

take mine. We form two spindles and run for it. Even if it is that powerful, they won't pursue us all the way back to New Edinburgh."

"You can run if you wish", Sturgeon said. "You're the heir now, so you have that prerogative. I'm standing and fighting."

"Are you suicidal?"

"Your plan implies that half of us won't go home, Cousin. I'm merely guaranteeing which half has to die."

Ireton's Executive Officer stepped into frame and whispered into his ear, saying something that made Ireton punch the arm of his chair.

"My father will understand", Sturgeon said. "As will yours."

"Die well, Cousin." Ireton said, and the comlink shut off. "Reform the fleet. Spindle formation, we're making a break for it."

Sturgeon gave the same reorganization order. "For God, Country, and the Duke!" he cried as his fleet engaged Zuzu in her robot. The massed naval fire did do some damage before she got close enough to respond by invoking Baal's Fire upon them all. As Ireton fled at best speed he wept for his cousin, and his brother, as Sturgeon's fleet disintegrated before Zuzu and *Minotaur*.

"You will be avenged!"

7 A DISINTERESTED BRIDEGROOM

The Red Eyes fleet emerged from hyperspace, returning in triumph to the planetoid-sized asteroid fortress known as Hell's Heart. Red Eyes, arrayed in all his finery, awaited them in the docking bay with a full honor guard about him and a crowd of fellow pirates ready to welcome home their haul-laden heroes.

Redalen's Revenge docked on one side, and *Great Gomorrah* on the other end, allowing both Dashing Jack and Zuzu the Painbringer the opportunity to walk with head held high as they disembarked from their vessels and strode with pride to meet their leader.

"Welcome home!" Red Eyes said. He held his arms open wide, saying "You have prevailed exactly as I knew you would."

Both of his lieutenants saluted. "Victory for Babylon!"

Red Eyes clapped Jack on the shoulders. "Your cool head and cunning kept the fleet together when things could have fallen apart. You also secured the great prize that this raid was all about. We are grateful, Jack, and you shall be rewarded for your daring."

Then Red Eyes went to his sister and did the same. "Your killer instincts served you well, as I knew they would, and you not only kept the worst threat at bay long enough for Jack to secure the prize, but when the right moment came you delivered the death stroke to the Ireton fleet and gutted them. You not only stole their hope to stop us but ripped out their hope for the future! That's something all of the galaxy will remember!"

Zuzu broke out cackling like an old witch. "We gutted them all right! How long until we attack again, High Admiral?"

"Soon, sister. For now, savor the delight of victory", Red Eyes said. "Now, Jack, where is the prize?"

Jack keyed into a comlink. "Gori, bring the master his presents."

At the point of a blaster, Gori prodded Countess Gabreila and Creton out of Revenge and down to the jubilant crowd. The braying mass of pirates first gasped as they beheld Gabriela, and then they erupted in lust-crazed obscenities that they hurled at her with mindless abandon. The vulgarity of their catcalls disgusted Gabreila so much that she couldn't conceal it, and that provoked a redoubling of them from the crowd.

Creton, looking on, stared in astonishment at the savagery on display remembering only that his father and Ramsey had sometimes remarked that some men were men in name only. Those were just words until now, and he felt a rage swell within him that he struggled to contain, one that did not go unnoticed.

"Courage, Creton", Gabriela said softly, taking his hand, "we need to endure this, for now, for their sake."

Now Red Eyes took a good look at what his lieutenants won in his stead. "At last, the Songbird of Second Salisbury is mine."

Gabriela looked at the blue-skinned, blood-red maned, half-man towering over her and Creton at half again a grown man's height. "Not for long."

"Long enough, my lady, as you shall soon realize", Red Eyes said as he approached them. "Jack, I see that you and Zuzu brought me a plaything."

"High Admiral, this is the page of Lord Roland." Jack said.

Red Eyes went down on one knee to get a better look at the boy. "Oh-ho!" Red Eyes, seizing Creton's head with one hand, "And I can see that the Guard's knights select boys with spirit."

Creton struck out at Red Eyes' arm. "Let go of me!"

Red Eyes smirked at the boy. "Flung about like a toy, still in bandages, and yet you would dare raise a hand against me? You are as brave as your master, boy, and just as foolish. I'll keep you with our noble guest here. It will keep both of you easier to manage until the matters in play are resolved."

Red Eyes drew blood on Creton's head to make the point plain, cutting the boy on either side of the face with his taloned hands. "That should ensure your quiescence until I am satisfied with greater things."

Then Red Eyes took his attention back to Gabriela. "And you shall remain in charge of the boy until I am ready to dispose of you. Mark this, my lady; while you must remain unspoiled, the boy has no such protection. Whatever I would otherwise do to you shall be done to him in your stead."

Gabriela gasped. "You wouldn't dare! Monster."

Red Eyes, without looking away from her, backhanded Creton and drew more blood from him- this time the corner of his mouth. "Does that answer you?"

Creton fell to the floor with a thump, provoking peels of laughter from the crowd of pirates assembled, laughter like the howls of hyenas. Gabriela pulled Creton to his feet, slowly, and saw the boy's face flash with anger for a moment.

"As God is my witness, I will kill you." Creton whispered, faintly, and that too caught Gabriela off-guard, but she also noticed that no one else heard it.

Red Eyes nodded to Jack, who in turn looked to Gori and said. "Take them to the guest chambers."

Creton, despite still being about half of Gabriela's height, shrugged off her attempt to carry him. "I can walk."

Something else now hit Gabriela in her gut, a mix of dread and resolve. As Gori lead them to their prison cell, she felt apprehensive as she noticed that Hell's Heart seemed filled with the degenerates that greeted her and Creton at the dock, degenerates that left them alone only because they feared the man leading them. Yet she was not fearful for her own sake, but for Creton's.

I cannot bear to see Roland die twice. Gabriela admitted in her heart, *Until we can escape, or we meet our fates, I shall care for him as I would for Roland. I won't stand before God as a cowardess when I could soothe the pain, cure what ails, or mend what is broken. Mother Mary, help me.*

* * *

On New Edinburgh, news of the Ireton fleet disaster at Dara's Folly reached Scarborough Castle. Flanked by his new heir, Count Samuel, Duke Ireton approached Sibley as he emerged from the Infirmary.

"Sibley, where is Lord Roland?" Duke Ireton said.

"Your Grace shall find my lord at prayer in the Chapel", Sibley said. "Shall I summon him?"

Ireton shook his head. "No, this I must discuss privately."

"We've heard", Sibley said. "I offer my condolences, Your Grace."

Ireton nodded. "My family and I are grateful, good Sibley, and we pray that your son is yet alive after this."

"Allow me to go with you to the Chapel, Your Grace." Sibley said, looking over to Count Samson, "This is a day for men to seek friends."

Ireton thought a moment, then said "Yes. That is a wise thing to do today."

Together they walked across the way to the nearby Chapel, where two Ireton men stood guard. They saluted at the approach of their duke.

"Everyone else is to remain outside, save for Father Martin and Bishop Cromwell." Ireton said, and then he went inside. At the altar, still wearing his undershirt, Ramsey knelt in prayer. Ireton could hear the old Latin, making out pleas to Mary, to the Archangels--the real ones, not Ramsey's superiors--and to several saints as he approached.

"Who approaches?" Ramsey said.

"Your host, Lord Roland." Ireton said, "I wish to speak with you, privately."

"There is no one here but you, I, and God." Ramsey said, "If this space pleases you."

"I would see the face of whom I address."

Ramsey slowly got to his feet. Even with the shirt on, the sun coming in through the stained-glass windows shined on Ramsey's back to show several scars where the blaster struck him. "Are you ready to fight, my lord?"

Ramsey turned to face Ireton. "I am."

"You know of what has happened while you were in recovery."

"Yes, Your Grace. Once I knew of the dispatch, I came here. It was the only useful thing I could do. I am sorry to hear of your son, your nephew, and the many men under their command."

"Samuel's report made it conclusive that the entire thing was a trap from the beginning, meant to intimidate us and dissuade further action against the pirates."

"What does Your Grace intend to do next?"

"Even with you at our side, we are diminished. My vassals already counsel for parley, preferring to pay a ransom over facing that monstrous machine again, and the Archduke is displeased that Countess Gabriela got abducted by those pirates while in my care. I am willing to fight, and my remaining sons are willing to fight, but-"

Ramsey held up a hand. "-something has forced your hand, hasn't it?"

"Count Vikuun Qis has brought this before the Court of Stars."

* * *

The Court of Stars, the galaxy's chamber where the domains of Mankind discuss the matters they share, meets once more in its chambers in Rome on Earth. Into the circular hall Count Vikuun Qis stepped arrayed in his most formal attire.

"Master Speaker," Qis said, "if I may."

The Speaker for the Court, an old man from one of the Chinese domains, nodded at him. "The Court recognizes Count Qis, speaking for the Grand Duchy of Gustavus."

Qis strode into the center of the chamber. All eyes, both those present and the magnitudes more watching remotely, were now focused upon him. Using the console before him, Qis began a holographic display presentation.

"My noble lords, the event we feared since His Grace Duke Kawamori gave his address this past Christmas has come to pass. Word by now has come to you of the raid upon New Edinburgh by the Red Eyes pirates. They came in a great fleet, massing thousands of their original mecha in many original starships."

"They used a great distraction of weaponized asteroids to screen their approach and draw the garrison away, then attacked from a second opposite direction to cause a panic and begin an orbital battle. The orbital battle allowed their battleship, containing their marines and elite squadron, to raid

Scarborough Castle and abduct my most noble cousin, Countess Gabriela Robin of Second Salisbury."

"In the course of the battle, not only did House Ireton suffer severe casualties among its garrison, but the household itself suffered great losses. The Keeper of the Seal turned out to be a traitor in league with the pirates, and it is he who gave the pirates all the intelligence needed to conduct such a perfect assault."

"The Lord Marshall died protecting his duke, and the Keeper died when his treachery got revealed. Countess Gabriela's party suffered injury in attempting to defend her, as did the duke and Lord Roland of the Solar Guard."

Qis heard several gasps from the crowd above.

"Lord Roland would have succeeded in his attempt to stop my cousin's abduction, but the Keeper shot him in the back at the last moment when Lord Roland's attention focused entirely on the villain leading the assault, the notorious pirate captain, Dashing Jack!"

Qis paused to let that sink in.

"Lord Roland shall recover presently, but while he convalesced Duke Ireton ordered a counterattack. This turned out to be a trap, and what decided it was this."

Qis now showed a mockup of *Minotaur* emerging on top of *Prince Charles* and laying waste to the Ireton fleet.

"Red Eyes plotted this monstrous butchery in the aim to intimidate not just House Ireton, or the Grand Duchy of New Scotland, but all of the galaxy. He needs us cowering in fear while he makes a bold violation of my cousin's virtue to satisfy his savage scheme. I ask you, good men of Christendom, come now to war upon this monster before it is too late!"

Qis paused again. He listened for the signs, for words of concurrence, before continuing and got them.

"Noble lords of all Christendom, lay aside your disputes and come together. You have all beheld my cousin's beauty with your own eyes and ears, so would you see it spoiled by that inhuman barbarian and laid to waste? Only Almighty God knows to what end Red Eyes intends to put her virtue, her life, even her immortal soul in his own quest for power and lust for plunder."

"This tragedy need not come to pass! Take up your swords, mount your mecha, and mass your fleets in the name of the Songbird of Second Salisbury! House Ireton may be too proud to call for aide, but I--speaking not only for my own family, but hers--am yet a humble servant and so I will not refuse the aide of good Christians against such heretics and blasphemers."

The Speaker stepped in. "My lord has made his proposal clear. The question is before this assembly. Shall we petition His Holiness to issue a Call To Arms or not?"

The signs marking the ruling dynasties of Mankind, the Grand Duchies of

Galactic Christendom, now began to shift from their neutral yellows to either a go-call of green or a no-call of red. Not one refrained. Not one denied. Soon a solid stream of green lit up the chamber. Qis smiled at the result.

"The proposal is passed." The Speaker smiled at Qis, "Does my lord have such a petition prepared?"

"I do, Master Speaker." Qis said, and handed the Speaker his written proposal. The Speaker skimmed it.

"My noble lords, the proposal as written is as spoken. By assent, I shall enter it without further action."

Again, swiftly the lights turned green. "It is so done. We shall have our response from the Holy Father presently. Is there any comment to be had?"
A hologram of an Italian man appeared. "The Court recognizes Duke Uno, speaking for the New Roman League."

"We have faith that the Holy Father shall accept and grant the noble lord's petition. The League offers to send our vanguard unit, the Knights of the Eagle, to the assembled force as soon as the Holy Father grants that petition. As House Ireton is in need, we come in brotherly love to support them against these invaders and make viable a second rescue fleet."

Qis smiled. "My noble father as well as my cousin is humbled by the League's offer of aide. I know it is but the first of many, as I believe that many of you shall share this desire for justice and be ready to come across the galaxy to see it done."

And they did. Many such offers came, in many forms, some material and some not. But the one all expected came not long after the proposal's passage. The Speaker received a message.

"The Solar Guard shall come."

All the chamber cheered.

* * *

Qis departed from Rome in a diplomatic skycar, flying North to the ancestral homeland of his family in Scandinavia. Landing in Oslo, Norway, he arrived at the family's home on Earth. The servants welcomed him home. As the footman took his cloak, he addressed the majordomo. "All is as I specified, Robert?"

Robert, an old family retainer, smiled and nodded. "Your meal is being delivered to your office presently, my lord. Your recent purchase from New Edinburgh worked out nicely."

Qis smiled and put a gloved hand on the old man. "Your timing remains impeccable. As soon as I am finished, I am not to be disturbed until I say otherwise."

"Very good, my lord." Robert said, and Qis took leave of him and the others. He walked up the stairs and into the secure wing of the house, where he kept his office on Earth, and as he entered the chambers, he saw a boy about Creton's age next to a delivery cart arranging his meal.

Qis kept quiet, watching the boy a moment execute his duty, making note of the lad's eagerness to ensure he did exactly as told. Only when the boy turned around to leave did he notice Qis standing there.

"My lord!" he said, quickly bowing, "Your meal is ready."

Qis smirked at him. "I see. Hold a moment, lad."

Qis took his seat at the table prepared. He looked over the food and drink arrayed: a modest plate of fresh fruit next to a warm sandwich, a bowl of soup, and a cup of tea. He then waived the boy over.

"You're far too nervous, my boy, and such nerves ruins a lad's character quickly." Qis said as he handed the boy the cup, "By my permission, have some tea. It will calm you."

The boy bowed and took the cup. "Thank you, my lord." he said, and took a long sip. The boy handed the cup back, and a moment passed.

"Better?" Qis looked on, as if expecting something.

The boy's eyes went wide in surprise, and his chested seized up. Then he collapsed, looking upon Qis with an arm outstretched. Qis took it and went down on one knee.

Qis said, "You are one more sacrifice I make for what Mankind requires: the unity of a King of Kings, all speaking the same tongue that speaks the same creed, the creed of Babylon."

Moments later, the serving boy went limp and Qis keyed into the comlink. "Robert, another attempted averted. Arrange for the boy's funeral. Pay out from the household budget."

"I presume that there is a suspect, my lord?"

"Yes, Robert. As you noted, my recent purchase did nicely. For now, brew some coffee and bring it up. It's going to be a long night."

"Very good, my lord."

* * *

After dark, Qis drew the shades and locked the door. Drawing a hood over his head and covering part of his face, he sat in his chair and activated a holographic projector. Some moments later, a miniature image of Red Eyes, kneeling, appeared.

"Master", Red Eyes said, "your plan resolved exactly as you claimed. We have the countess, we demoralized House Ireton, and the duke is now facing dissent from his vassals as well as criticism from his lord."

"Very good, High Admiral."

"We also debuted the two new designs in this action, both of which met expectations. We shall proceed with further combat tests, but we are confident that we can turn these designs around into their mass-produced counterparts by this time next year."

"Good, good." Qis said, "Now, the matter of the Countess. Has she be rendered to our client yet?"

"No, master. She came with Lord Roland's page, and until we can render her to him, we are using the boy to control her."

Qis's face went into a frown. "She must be disposed of promptly, High Admiral! Has the client not come to take possession yet?"

"He is immersed in the work we engaged him to do. Timeliness is sometimes lost on him." Red Eyes said, "But we are secure in Hell's Heart. We may travel at-will should we deign to do so."

"Your pride in your engineering is evident, High Admiral, as in your achievement in turning a bunch of desperate and grasping cutthroats into a viable armada. You shall soon be put to the test on both points."

"Oh?"

"The Countess's cousin went to the Court of Stars. He pleaded for the houses of Mankind to rally to Ireton's aide and come forth against you."

"And they're coming?"

"They are. How many is not yet known, but it will be in the days to come, but I do know this: The Solar Guard comes. Not just Lord Roland. They're sending at least one battleship against you, and now that they committed forces others will follow. You shall see a fleet of allied houses coming against you, led by many worthy fighting men of Christendom, and they desire to take back the prize you possess."

"That will be quite a test for the armada, Master." Red Eyes said with a toothy grin, "I look forward to it."

"Be certain to conclude the matter before that fleet finds you and comes for you. You shall not get a second chance if you fail to do so now."

"It will be done, Master." Red Eye said, "We are more than enough for whatever those fools array against us. They are a disunited rabble, and we are a unified force. We shall break their bonds and destroy them one by one."

"Make good on that boast." Qis said, "Or you're done."

"Victory For Babylon!" Red Eyes said and signed off.

* * *

Scarborough Castle and the nearby military spaceport swarmed with workers removing rubble and engaging in repairs. The funerals and wakes went on for a week straight, both on the surface and in orbit, but the affairs of state never cease, and so Duke Ireton met with Ramsey in the castle's Armory to discuss those very affairs.

"Ah, Lord Roland." Ireton said, now standing with a cane. "Good of you to come promptly. We have a call from Earth."

Ramsey recognized the sigil in the holographic display. "From Palatine

Hill, specifically. This is a Guard transmission."

"Put it through." Ireton ordered, and the display became that of an old man in a Guard uniform like Ramsey's, only bearing the sign of Archangel Michael. Ramsey saluted, and Duke Ireton nodded.

"Your Grace, Roland", Duke Michael said, "I'm glad to get to you before the word from the Court next door spread."

"We are aware of Count Qis's plea, Your Grace", Ireton said, "Did the Holy Father do as we expect?"

"Yes, he did."

"What has come after that became known?" Ramsey said, "Your Grace has to have some knowledge of that."

"The New Roman League, the True Middle Kingdom, and the Grand Duchy of New Prussia have all committed forces so far. The Guard will dispatch a battleship with escorts to the effort."

"Which one?" Ramsey said, curious.

"*Oklahoma.* It turns out that her captain is a fan."

"Of the Countess?" Ireton said.

"Of your guest." Michael chuckled.

"We've worked together before." Ramsey said, "I think you'll get along well with him, Your Grace."

"Altogether," Michael said, "we're looking at a fleet of a thousand ships and six thousand mecha of various kinds, and we're not done yet. The New Romans are hot for taking revenge upon Dashing Jack."

"Will there be a formal declaration of Anathema upon the Red Eyes pirates?" Ramsey said.

"That is will be discussed in an hour or so, but I think we shall see it. That will open the flood gates and many more will come to battle."

"That threatens issues of discipline, Your Grace." Ireton said, "Without clear authority, coordination in battle will fall apart swiftly, and Red Eyes is more than cunning enough to notice that before the fact and exploit it to terrible effect. We cannot repeat Dara's Folly."

"I concur." Ramsey said, "It is His Grace Ireton's duty to see that handled, but it must be handled before the dispatch. In the meantime, we have the other pressing matter to handle."

"The one we've avoided until now?"

"Yes, Your Grace." Ramsey said, pulling up a map of the nearby space, "We lost contact with both the Countess and the pirates when they left Dara's Folly. We don't know where they are, yet, but I think we have a means to find that out."

"There is?" Ireton said, and then the fact came back to the fore of his mind, "Of course! The transmitter."

"Meaning that my page, Creton, is alive." Ramsey said, "And that is more than good news for us."

"What gives you such confidence?" Michael said.

"First, the fact that the frequency used is not one of ours." Ramsey said, "That means Jack wanted it that way, and if Jack wanted it that way then he's playing an angle of his own that Red Eyes may not even know of. Second, that the Countess used it means that she found it and used it from concealment. As she is no lightfoot or coin-flicher, she had to get it while searching someone unconscious. As there would be no one else she could safely search than Creton, it had to be one found on him, one planted just before while being bandaged by Jack's doctor. Third, we can reason Creton being alive by the Countess needing to be had without despoiling her. We know her demeanor, so if she is to be controlled then Jack must turn her good heart against her by using Creton as a proxy for punishment, which he cannot be if he is dead."

"So they beat or flog the boy instead of her? How vile." Ireton said.

"If that is all they do to him in her stead, then both are fortunate", Michael said. "In any case our time is limited. Such women as the Countess are stolen away to satisfy specific monsters for specific purposes, and we can reasonably assume that she shall soon be sacrificed if we cannot find her location and get her out of the hands of her captors."

"Sibley and I shall soon depart to attempt a signal trace." Ramsey said, "We'll start at Dara's Folly and follow along the pirate's last known trajectory. While we do that, we'll check for that frequency as well as the one assigned to the transmitter that Creton had issued to him. If either he or the Countess respond, so much the better, but we're planning upon picking up the signal and following that to wherever their base is this time."

"And then?" Ireton said.

"Oh, he'll calmly assess the situation at hand before reporting back with the enemy's location", Michael said with a smile.

"And then you'll attempt some foolhardy heroic plan to rescue her." Ireton said with a laugh.

"Your Graces wound me with your insinuations." Ramsey said, feigning offense, "I shall certainly attempt a logical and well-reasoned plan to rescue the Countess, after I do my duty to report the location of the pirates' base of operations back here to Scarborough Castle."

"If you were anyone else, I would be concerned." Michael said, "Fortunately Sibley will be with you, so I know that everything will end well."

Ireton held up both hands. "Your Grace, my lord, I must end this discussion now that the matter is handled. May God be with you, Your Grace."

"And also with you." Michael said before signing off.

"That was your master, wasn't it?" Ireton said, looking at Ramsey.

"Indeed, Your Grace. His Grace the Duke of the Seat of Archangel Michael was my mentor and predecessor."

Ireton slapped Ramsey on the back and laughed. "I see!"

"Then you know that all is in good hands, Your Grace. By your leave."

"Go forth, Lion of the Guard. Find our songbird."

Ramsey bowed. "May you bring order to chaos before my return, Your Grace." he said, and then he left for the spaceport where Sibley awaited him in *Baden-Powell.*

8 A ROMANTIC COMPLICATION

Gabriela hushed Creton as she inspected his bandages. "Enough of that. You're still injured, and you can't help yourself if you don't heal properly."

Creton frowned as Gabriela poked and prodded, making him grimace when she pressed against one of the heavy bruises or had him stretch his limbs.

"You're not a man yet", she said, "however much you try to act the role, and being defiant only makes it more likely that you will not go home at all instead of merely needing a doctor."

Now she moved in closer and whispered into his ear. "I took your transmitter and used it to warn the Ireton fleet, but they still got destroyed. I don't know what else to do."

This confession nearly caught Creton off-guard, but he turned his face away from the viewscreen just in case as if she prodded him someplace sore again. "My lady, I still have it. What are you talking about?"

Gabriela seemed confused for a moment, then said "It's not on your belt?"

"No, hidden in my boots."

"Have you used it?"

"No."

"Then let's get it working." She stood up and reached for his feet, speaking up again. "Off with these, lad. I'll not have you losing toes."

In a few moments she removed them and handed them to Creton. Then she stood over him, her back to the viewscreen. "Now let's look at those cuts on your head."

Creton took the moment to slip into the secret compartment of a boot, removed the transmitter therein. "I can set a signal with this for them to track." he whispered.

"Do it." she answered. Creton set the transmitter to play as a tracking beacon before replacing into his boot.

Again, speaking up, Gabriela backed away from Creton. "Well, aside from a change of bandages and a bath, you're find for now."

Creton put his boots back on, and then stood to his feet to get them just right again. She took him by the hands and knelt. Creton followed her lead, knowing that this again allowed frank, if whispered, talk.

"Do you know the range on that transmitter?" Gabriela asked.

"I've never had to use it before, so I don't know."

"Let's hope it's got better range that whatever it is I found on you."

"It's tied to Guard-specific frequency bands, so if my lord comes looking and he's close enough, it will come up clear as a church bell."

"What about this one I have then?"

"If they find this place, there's bound to be an alert of some sort." Creton said, "If you transmit then, they'll know for certain they have the right place."

"That's good."

"My lady, we should come up with a plan to escape anyway. Even if my lord comes, he still has to get to us. If we can meet him halfway, or get outside, then he can pick us up and withdraw to safety before reinforcements can stop him and us."

* * *

Azazel, in his workshop, noticed a notification sound on his console. Curious, he looked at it, and found it coming from the prison wing. No guards or other personnel came forth to investigate it, so he activated his back door into Hell's Heart's security system and looked for himself. There he saw Gabriela and Creton apparently kneeling in prayer, but the angel knew without thought that this was a ruse because he felt none of the familiar tension of prayer coming from them.

Curious indeed, he thought as he isolated the signal into another window and began a trace, *this isn't the one that Red Eyes' man Jack planted.*

The trace completed seconds later, identifying a signal beyond what is known in the Red Eyes Armada, but coming from a device in the boy's boot.

Oh, this could be interesting. If none of them didn't find it, then I see no reason to volunteer that information. Let's see the data stream.

Azazel looked at the breakdown of where the transmitter aimed itself and found a few minutes later that Earth was the target, which made the angel chuckle.

Of course. Azazel thought. Then he turned his attention to Gabriela and ran the scan of her that he'd been meaning to do. The readout pleased him, as she was not only a young woman in perfect health and peak fertility but possessed of a genetic record he sought. She had the markers he desired to complete his own ambitions.

She is indeed a worthy bride. These mortals have done well, but I sense resistance on her part. That will not do.

Azazel looked over at another window, where he monitored the manufacturing quarter. The Goblin line's retooling into producing Hobgoblins was on schedule. The prototype lab's tooling to fast-produce the new elite model was also on schedule. The shipyard wing's retooling of a second line to produce a new ship class remained on schedule, and the refit and upgrade of *Minotaur* was complete.

Turning back to the prison cell camera, he saw the pair had finished their false prayers.

They think they can thwart this plan? Oh, this should be entertaining indeed. I think this is a good opportunity to see my bride's quality in action, but first some insurance. I don't want my property damaged, Azazel thought.

He left his workshop, taking the form of one of the many pirates as a disguise. He made his way to the brig, where he took the place of the man assigned to feed the prisoners.

"Meal time." Azazel said. He opened the cell, wheeled in their meal, and handed both food and drink to Gabriela and Creton. Into Gabriela's drink he put a drop of his essence, and she did not notice the adulteration as she drank the vessel dry. They said nothing to him, but just handed back dishes and vessels as they finished with them. He left as he came, but as he backed out, he saw with his inhuman eyes that his mark now lay about the Countess.

It's only a little something, he thought, but it is still a mark that my peers are inclined to trespass shall respect, and that will do for now.

* * *

Ramsey and Sibley launched *Baden-Powell* from the military spaceport beside Scarborough Castle. As they ascended through the atmosphere of New Edinburgh, they kept note of the coming noble houses committing to crush the Red Eyes Armada. Battleships, carriers, cruisers, destroyers, corvettes, frigates, and scores upon scores of escorting mecha appeared one after the next out of hyperspace and it was all Ireton could do to maintain order in the orbital traffic.

"That's a lot of men coming to defend one lady's honor", Sibley said.

"When it's our era's Helen of Troy, I can't be surprised at the response", Ramsey said.

"Course plotted to Dara's Folly", Sibley said. "Ready to go."

"Let's get away from this, Sibley, before some hot-head starts a dispute."

Sibley threw forward a lever and the ship accelerated to top speed, throwing *Baden-Powell* forward and away from New Edinburgh's orbit in moments. Maneuvering just over the plane of battle, they made for Dara's Folly. By doing so they avoided most of the debris left by the battle while allowing them to survey the site of the disastrous loss.

"Bring up the report", Ramsey said. Sibley threw the after-action report on the main screen as an overlay.

"Advance to the point where *Prince Charles* heard from the scout ship."

In conjunction with a smaller local map on another screen, the overlay showed a directional arrow depicting the direction of the transmission, on the far side of the belt. They passed an Ireton Ferguson-class cruiser, the *MacLeod*, anchored right outside the facility as they followed the transmission with naught said but a passcode sent, and acknowledgment received.

"I don't envy those men." Sibley said, "Having to garrison that accursed facility must chafe at them."

"Their Chaplain is a busy man." Ramsey said, "Ah-hah! We're here. Full stop."

Sibley brought *Baden-Powell* to a stop where the report put the initial signal.

"Overlay Jack's ship on this location, bow pointing towards the Ireton fleet."

Sibley did so, and Ramsey compared the rest of the battle report to this position on the main screen. "I think I see how this concluded, Sibley. Which way did the last records of the transmitter point?"

Sibley put it up on screen, and then he turned *Baden-Powell* on that course, advancing now at a slower cruising speed until the record cut off. Then he brought up a stellar map of the Dire March, marking all the systems and stellar phenomena along that trajectory.

"This was their largest and most ambitious raid. I doubt they wanted to dispatch that far from their base", Sibley said. "Yet we know that they often operate out of some prepared forward position."

"You have both frequencies set in the system, Sibley?"

"Of course. If they're transmitting on either, we'll pick it up."

Ramsey looked at the map, and his eyes came upon one with a massive asteroid belt avoided by commercial transit routes. "There, that's the best candidate. Why risk a planetary blockade when you have a proven capacity at adapting planetoids and asteroids into habitable locations?"

"An easily escapable headquarters for a pirate fleet? Of course!" Sibley said, setting the coordinates.

"Bring us right at the edge of the belt, Sibley. If they're there, then we won't need to go into that field to find them."

Sibley spun up *Baden-Powell*'s hyperdrive, and into hyperspace she went.

"There's another reason for Red Eyes to prefer a field or belt to a planetary base", Sibley said. "If he truly is someone with a significant manufacturing capacity, one he conceals in such a location is also one right next to a vast supply of raw materials. Out on the frontier of Christendom, that's as much a strategic as a logistical decision."

"Build a fleet in secret. Build an army in secret. Can probably organize enough asteroids and planetoids to mitigate or eliminate the need to raid for food or water with hydroponics and water recycling, combined with finding nearby stellar ice sources. For one like him, I doubt he'll shift to holding planets until he somehow builds a fleet able to take and hold them."

Baden-Powell emerged from hyperspace, right as Ramsey directed, and immediately the Solar Guard frequency lit up.

"That's got to be Creton", Sibley said, and he brought the signal up on screen. "It's operating as a beacon. That's a good lad!"

Ramsey clapped Sibley's shoulder. "And that means we've found them both. Let's verify that location before we send back the coordinates."

They brought *Baden-Powell*'s thrusters up again and carefully navigated the belt. Sibley put the sensors into a passive mode to reduce the odds of detection, as both men knew that Red Eyes would order Goblins out on patrol.

"It will likely be the biggest rock in the belt", Ramsey said. "We need not get eyes on it. We need only to get the signal close to that rock."

"You're going to get your wish, my lord", Sibley said. "Found the largest rock, and our trace is taking us there. Just a few moments longer until we can confirm that this is the location."

"We've got patrols coming from several directions", Ramsey said. "Hold on while I weave through them."

Ramsey took the controls and played a dangerous game of Cat & Mouse with the patrolling Goblin flights, using sensor shadows and timed movements to skirt around them as they closed. He maneuvered out from behind a larger asteroid, and the signal locked on.

"Got it, my lord", Sibley said.

"Check the other band", Ramsey said.

Sibley switched over to the other band, but nothing came through.

"Ping it", Ramsey said. Sibley sent one ping on the line, one ping only.

A moment later a faint whisper came on the line. "Who's there?"

"It's her." Sibley said.

Ramsey keyed in. "This is Roland. I've got your location. Hold on. I'm coming for you."

Sibley contacted New Edinburgh and passed on the coordinates for the Red Eyes' Pirates base.

* * *

"Gori," Jack said, "while I'm in the meeting with the boss go check on our leverage. Don't talk. Just monitor. We'll discuss what you find after this."

"Aye, Captain." Gori said, and Jack entered the Grand Hall where he found Red Eyes, Zuzu, and Azazel waiting for him.

"About time, Captain." Zuzu said.

"I got the notification while in the middle of a private session in the Pillow

Ward", Jack said. "I could not disengage so easily."

Jack crossed the hall and took a space in a semi-circle about the raised throne where Red Eyes sat. A portable holographic projector sat in the middle. Red Eyes slapped the misshapen toady beside his throne, and the wretch turned it on.

"We can count on our enemies coming for us soon." Red Eyes stood up and paced about the throne. "This is what will be done."

Red Eyes waved at the toady, and he expanded the image to be that of Hell's Heart and the belt around it.

"As I speak, men in Goblins sortie into the belt to mine the likely approaches. They will also put beacons on certain asteroids, which will be used to mark the ranges for the gunnery crews. Those crews are now mapping out their sectors of the belt, preparing to make the most of their cannons and missiles when the attack comes."

"I presume that this is meant to make the most of our resources." Jack said, "If we face a proper reprisal, they will come in great force and from multiple approaches. In that case, withdrawal is our only viable option, Minotaur or not."

"That still takes time." Zuzu said, "Even if we begin spinning up the hyperdrive upon detection, we'll be under fire before we can escape."

"Those drives are as good as they can be, for now." Azazel said, "As is everything else here. I've automated most of it, and the rest can be handled by any of you in my stead."

"Azazel here will leave presently. He's going to solve the problem our manufacturing will soon make too apparent, which is a lack of manpower, and that requires the erection of a facility that we cannot hold here." Red Eyes smiled at the revelation, as he saw the signs of surprise on his lieutenants' faces, "With him shall go the prize we risked and plotting so much to acquire, but first we must send him off properly."

"Properly?" Jack said, "This means some pageantry, doesn't it?"

"It does." Azazel said, "It is necessary to fulfill the contract. Your Master and the High Admiral accepted this clause previously, so it's not a matter of if, but when it shall be done."

"And you imply that this is about the girl?" Zuzu said.

"Yes. The fulfillment of the contract requires that the transfer be in the lawful fashion, and that means a proper marriage ceremony."

Jack and Zuzu looked at Azazel as if he were drunk.

"The next project required a fulfilled contract." Red Eyes said, "So it shall be done. I expect that any reprisal shall come while we conclude this affair, so neither of you shall be required to attend. Instead you two shall be ready to sortie when they come at us. I shall conduct the ceremony under my authority as High Admiral, and this place being my ship in particular. You'll have your bride, angel."

*　*　*

"The boy sleeps again." Gabreila said, softly, as she sat next to Creton's slumbering form, "His wounds drain him terribly."

Gori, outside the cell, handed the man tasked with watching over her a bottle. "Get some sandwiches and be quick about it."

The pirate took a long pull off the bottle, wiped his chin, and then stood. "Aye, Commander."

Gori watched as the pirate scurried out of the brig and towards the nearest dispensary. He pulled up another chair, a bigger one, for him and his kind, before he adjusted the display showing Gabriela. She looked into the far corner, put her head in her hand, and began to sing.

It was a song in the older tongues, a tongue that Gori did not know. She sang it slow, with a tone that struck Gori as somewhere between insistent and infatuated. It captured Gori's attention complete, having him now stare as the monitor as if caught up in an old feature film.

He took notice that many of the qualities he'd been told were most desirable now came forth. In her singing, Gabriela expressed a beauty that Gori found lacking in his own life and surroundings. He saw a delicate grace in Gabriela's movements, as she now got up to dance about the cell as the song increased in intensity of passion and contrasted this with those of the few women, he knows well enough to compare.

Even now, confined and confounded, she held this power of beauty in her heart and used song to bring it forth. She was not just a notable noblewoman now, but a living paragon of something deeper and stronger than anything Gori had beheld before.

"Now the value is apparent." Gori said, "This is not just a matter of terror and morale. This is a matter of quality."

The pirate lackey returned. "Sir, your sandwiches", he said. Then shook Gori when the giant didn't respond right away.

"Ah, there you are. Take one and eat."

"That happens to everyone if you're not careful." The pirate took a sandwich and poured himself some more from the bottle. "'Sirens' they call 'em back then. Very dangerous."

"Does she sing often?"

"When the boy sleeps. She does it when she's alone and unable to sleep herself. Watch! She'll soon lay down and rest herself."

Gori now remembered that no one ever took the planted transmitter off of her. Ah, clever, Gori thought, Intermittent singing on the frequency in hopes of getting a response, and then have them home in on it to track her down.

"Does she sing anything common?" Gori asked.

The pirate shook his head. "No, it's all in some tongue only priests and those like them known, I think. She'll go on for four or five minutes at a time, rest some, and repeat that a few times while the boy sleeps."

"He sleeps a lot?"

"If you got beat like that, you would too if you lacked a med bed."

Got you! Gori thought, looking at Gabriela.

* * *

Gori and Jack met back at their quarters, where they sealed the door and turned on their surveillance decoys. Gori poured a drink for both men.

"The High Admiral has to realize that our captives have transmitters and will do what they can to bring that reprisal to our doorstep", Gori said. "Captain, you know that he's getting carried away with demonstrating how brilliant he is with these operational plans. Why hasn't the Architect taking his prize already? I've seen first-hand that she is what he demands of a bride."

"Marriage, Gori", Jack said. He sighed and took a drink. "Whatever it is that allows him to do as we do, its key element is that he properly wed the woman first."

Gori slapped his forehead. "Of all the ridiculous things!"

"Zuzu shares that sentiment, for what it's worth", Jack took another drink. "But she's screwed. There's no way she'll ever have the presence of mind to cut ties and run when things go wrong. She has no sense of when a game goes against you, and she's very much a no-quitter type, as you saw firsthand."

"You're saying we should be looking to get out of here before this all blows up in our faces?"

"Exactly." Jack said as he pulled a project from his pocket. "Observe."

Jack tossed the projector on the table and brought up the map he saw in the closed meeting. "Red Eyes presumes that they're going to come, and soon. Zuzu pointed out that we can't escape without coming under fire, so Red Eyes has men laying mines and setting killzones for the fortress gunners. He's also going to transition to a four-shift duty cycle, with ship refit being prioritized so we can launch on short notice."

"Leave will be canceled, won't it?" Gori poured himself and Jack another drink.

"Of course. The men won't like it, but they'll get in line because they don't want to die."

"Do you think we can find a plausible angle to get out of this before they come?"

"What do you have in mind?"

"There's no way that the Architect will stick around."

Jack took another drink. "You're reading my mind. After that marriage ceremony, he's taking the Countess and going off to the High Admiral's next big project."

"The one about manpower? What does he know about recruitment?"

Jack shook his head. "It's not about recruiting, Gori. He makes things. That doesn't stop with machines."

Gori took a moment before he got the point. "The madman!"

"He's going to bring the Nephilim back, Gori. All of them. And he's going to use what would, by then, be his by right as the raw material necessary to make that happen."

"And the High Admiral?"

"Is fine with it, of course, because he thinks they'll listen to his orders."

Gori took a deep breath, and then emptied his glass. "We're running from this disaster, aren't we?"

"As soon as it's certain, yes."

* * *

Ramsey and Sibley clamped *Baden-Powell* upon a larger asteroid in the belt and powered down to minimal systems. The two men kept the coms open, now monitoring the pirates' traffic as they also monitored the frequencies used by Creton and Gabriela.

As more data came in, the two men added to and updated the map of the local area that they constructed. Soon they had all of the laid mines mapped out, and the range-marking beacons located and pegged. All the while, they had the pleasure of listening to Gabriela singing.

"You know she's singing to you, my lord", Sibley said.

"And apparently Creton isn't working quite as they had hoped", Ramsey said, "He's healing, but it's draining him."

"Especially with the food they would feed to him. It's a good thing that most of them will soon come before our Maker, as they would run at the wrath of his mother."

Ramsey smiled at the thought of Sibley's wife beating them with her cast-iron pan. "That they would."

Now a signal came in from outside the system. "Duke Ireton, I warrant." Sibley said.

Ramsey put it through and Ireton's head appeared on screen. "We've received your coordinates", Ireton said. "If you have any situation updates, now's the time."

"We're sending you a current map of the battlefield", Ramsey said, and he put out a quick burst back to New Edinburgh. "We've verified that both Countess Gabriela and my page are present and alive, but we also confirm that they have fortified a large planetoid. It's a well-armed colony, and they've been taking the time to mark out ranges in the surrounding asteroid belt."

"We have also reason to believe that they have preparations to flee in case of attack, though what those plans are or how they intend to achieve escape is not known to us, Your Grace", Sibley said. "There is the curious concern that the Countess remains confined to a cell instead of passed along to whomever claims her, which may yet give us a window to act."

"Are you two prepared to embark on an attempt to rescue her from their clutches before we arrive?"

"He is, Your Grace", Sibley said. "I'm far too old for such things."

"I'm going out alone and on foot", Ramsey said. "They're looking for ships and mecha, not men, and certainly not a lone man. I will infiltrate from a side airlock, make my way to the brig, and liberate the Countess and my page. Then we shall escape, likely back the way I came, and exfiltrate from the belt once we're back aboard my ship. Then we return to New Edinburgh, and the way is clear to not only assault Red Eyes' space fortress, but to destroy it and all within it without concern for anything but the villains' escape."

"My lord is confident of success", Ireton said. "Let us hope that your adventure succeeds before we dispatch in 12 hours."

Ramsey nodded. "So do I."

9 TO HELL'S HEART WE GO

Duke Ireton looked out as his shuttle took off from the military spaceport. Beside him sat his son Samuel, the heir's attention captured by a tablet feeding him ongoing information updates about the reprisal fleet.

"Father, *Oklahoma* reports that it is delayed and will not arrive in time to dispatch with us. Her captain requests that we go ahead without her."

"Unfortunate, but tolerable", Old Ireton said. He saw the clouds first thicken, and then thin out as they passed through them. "We have plenty of firepower without theirs, and we should be fine in their absence. They have the final coordinates, so they will meet us at the battlefield."

"And Mother?" Samuel said.

"She is where she can best help us now, son."

The two Iretons left it at that as their shuttle exited the atmosphere of New Edinburgh and entered orbital space. There they saw a vast and diverse array of battleships, carriers, cruisers, frigates, destroyers, corvettes, and mecha gathering at the mustering zone between Lagrange 1 and Lagrange 3. The shuttle flew around the gathered fleet, surveying the ships gathered with each one coming up on Samuel's tablet, before locking on to and approaching the grand flagship: *MacBeth*, a battleship, first of its class and elder sister to *Prince Charles*.

"We're forced to take the Old Play for our flagship", Old Ireton said. "This is not a good omen, son."

"I can't believe none of your brothers would send their battleships", Samuel said.

"If we weren't so pressed for time, I'd be able to deal with such insolence", Old Ireton said. "'Local security', what a fraud! I need them to come, and they refuse to get out of their chairs. Mark this, son. They see the death of your brother as a sign that we are weak, and they still resent me succeeding your grandfather instead of your uncle Charles, so it is no surprise that they wish to see me worn thin before they push to usurp your birthright for themselves."

Samuel sighed. "It is incredible that we can get the aide of noble lords from the far end of the galaxy, coming in the name of Christendom, but our own flesh and blood refused your call and feign local difficulty to justify their inaction."

The shuttle pilot now addressed them. "Your Grace, we're landing in *MacBeth*'s hangar bay."

Samson helped his father stand and escorted him off the shuttle, where they were met by the ship's Executive Officer.

"Welcome aboard, Your Grace", the Executive Officer saluted. "The Captain awaits you on the bridge."

Ireton looked at the man a moment, a Commander by his uniform. "It's 'Jefferson', isn't it?"

"Yes, Your Grace", Jefferson said with a beaming, prideful smile. "Commander Sir Johnathan Jefferson. My father is Lord of New Havershem and oversees your private hunting reserve."

"You've done well, Commander", Old Ireton said. He walked towards the lifts with his son and Jefferson beside him. "I still regret not attending your wedding."

"Your Grace's humility is inspiring", Jefferson said.

Now they entered the lift, and Jefferson keyed in for the bridge.

"Commander", Samson said, "what of the fleet's readiness?"

"So far the measures decreed to reduce friction to a minimum have held" Jefferson answered. "There's been some force-on-force skirmishing and wargaming, which has worked so far as intended, but councils have been less than effective until the intelligence came from Lord Roland."

"Speaking of which, I presume that the assorted fleet commanders await me?" Old Ireton said.

"Yes, Your Grace, but first the Captain wishes to speak with you", Jefferson said.

"Of course he does."

The lift arrived at the bridge. "Admiral on the bridge!" a crewman bellowed as Old Ireton stepped out on to the bridge. Samson and Jefferson followed. In the middle, a chair rotated around, and a middle-aged man stood and saluted. "God's Truth, Your Grace, you look like you ran ragged through Hell."

Old Ireton laughed. "And I am astounded that you kiss your wife with those lips."

Everyone glanced at each other, smiled, and nodded along as if understood what they witnessed. The two aging men embraced and clapped each other on the back.

"Now we're two old fools off to save a girl from a fate worse than death." Ireton said to the Captain, "Ready for one more adventure, Jerry?"

"Ready, Your Grace." The Captain offered Ireton his chair. As Old Ireton sat down, the Captain said, "Open coms to the fleet."

The Communications Officer complied. "You're on, Captain."

"This is Captain Count Gerald Denton, Captain of the battleship *MacBeth*. The Lord Admiral of the Fleet, His Grace the Duke of the Dire March, Sir Henry Ireton has arrived and has taken command. We are to depart from New Edinburgh presently. All commands are to attend a Council of War upon setting sail, according to fleet protocol."

Ireton followed. "My assembled lords, we go forth this day in lawful reprisal against the Red Eyes pirates in their criminal aggression against my people and their abduction of Christendom's living treasure, Countess Gabriela Robin. The Holy Father blesses our endeavor and prays not only for our victory in battle, but for the safe return of the Songbird of Second Salisbury. These heretics and barbarians are declared outlaws, to the last. Fear not to die, for this is a righteous cause. Dread not the matter of mercy, for they showed none and shall receive none. Care only for taking back what is ours."

Ireton looked at his old friend, who nodded at him.

"We launch. All ships, come about and make for the battlefield. Worry not for those left behind. They shall meet us there."

* * *

Ramsey, his armor donned, entered the dorsal airlock. "Sibley, I want you to stay in contact with the fleet and keep them informed of the situation as it develops."

"Yes, my lord", Sibley said, back in the cockpit. "Speaking of which, Ireton just launched the fleet. They'll be entering hyperspace presently, if Ireton follows his habit of command and holds a Council of War, so we can begin the countdown now. Make haste!"

Ramsey strapped on the rocket pack as he secured the airlock and depressurized. "Understood, Sibley. Do you have my tracking signal?"

"Loud and clear, my lord."

Ramsey opened the exterior hatch and stepped out on the hull. "All right then. Here I go!"

Ramsey released the magnets in his boots and pushed away from the hull, reorienting himself and igniting the rocket pack. Now he cruised away from *Baden-Powell* and through the asteroid belt. The comlink built into his off-hand's bracer fed the sensors from his ship into his helmet's field of view.

"Coms check", Ramsey said.

"Loud and clear, my lord."

"Good. Moving in."

Ramsey flitted from rock to rock, watching the scanner in his display, holding position when a patrolling Goblin got too close and proceeding once the way was clear. Slowly he crept up to that final gap between the rocks and the fortress, where he paused and observed the traffic looking for an ill-observed angle.

"Sibley, a little help if you would."

Sibley took the feed from Ramsey's helmet and compared them to the larger traffic going on. Seeing a void, he put a virtual marker into the map.

"There, my lord."

Ramsey saw an arrow appear in his view, pointing up and just over to the right. He moved upwards from rock to rock until the arrow leveled off. Then he shot across the gap and made the surface of Hell's Heart. Once on the outside, he skulked about until he found an airlock hatch.

"Sibley, I found a way in. I'm setting a beacon here." Ramsey took a stick about as long as his hand's width, set it against his comlink bracer, and waited for the notification that its signal activated. Then he fixed it into the airlock's frame.

"Coming in loud and clear, my lord", Sibley said. "The fleet's well on its way now."

"Effecting entry now."

Ramsey broke into the airlock, drawing beam sword and blaster while waiting on the repressurization to conclude, and when the inside seal opened, he saw two guards turning to face him.

"Surprise!" he said. He shot one and ran the other through, then tossed their bodies into the airlock pressurization chamber before closing it. Looking about, he saw a sign saying, "Manufacturing Wing, Outer Ring." Soon he found a map and oriented himself, finding that he had to pass through the Manufacturing Wing to get to the Brig, so he hit his comlink and tuned to Gabriela's transmitter.

"Gabriela, I'm here."

* * *

Zuzu slammed her fist upon the cell door. "I'm coming in!"

A moment later she threw open the cell door and walked in, seeing Gabriela standing while Creton slept on the nearby bed.

"My host must be consumed with his duties to send you in his stead", Gabriela said. "He must not trust his men to do what he sent you for."

Zuzu snapped her fingers and a toady entered the room with a golden dress on a hanger, which the toady hanged upon the wall using an open hook.

"My brother the High Admiral tells me that this business of ours shall be concluded shortly." Zuzu said, "Your groom is ready to receive you. Put on this dress, so you can meet your husband properly."

Gabriela looked at the dress, an impossibly fine garment that shone like pure gold while seemingly composed of spider silk and diamond dust.

Gabriela said, "But my father-"

"-is irrelevant. By right of conquest, my brother is your master now, and it is his will that you be given in marriage to the groom he's chosen for you." Zuzu looked over at Creton's sleeping form. "If you know what is good for you, you will do as your lord and master commands of you."

Gabriela looked at Zuzu's toothy grin and saw her rubbing her hands together as the blue-skinned giantess glanced at the boy.

"Am I not afforded the decency of privacy?"

Zuzu's smile widened. "A moment."

Zuzu snapped her fingers. The toady took the chair, moved it next to the monitor and then stood upon it so that he covered the screen while facing the wall. Gabriela, just in case, pulled the bedsheet over Creton's face and then she gave an expectant stare to Zuzu.

"You have nothing that I don't", Zuzu said. "Get on with it."

Gabriela responded by doffing her tabard, and with a dancer's whirl she spun up the force needed to hurl it up and over Zuzu's face. The giantess could only laugh at the display of defiant insistence upon modesty. "Be glad that your groom insists upon seeing you this way. If it were my brother, he would have shorn you of that frivolity when he branded his mark upon you and made you his concubine."

"Thank God for small mercies." Gabriela said as she changed into the gold dress.

"I wouldn't be so thankful. Don't mistake a slow hand for a soft one, girl. Your groom has grand designs for you, and he's seen enough of you to be quite insistent. Once his mind fixes upon a thing, he advances upon it like Death itself."

Gabriela finished the change and pulled the tabard off Zuzu's head. "I would expect frustration were I him."

"I wouldn't", Zuzu said as her eyes examined Gabriela as if the Countess were prey in a hunt. "He always gets his way."

* * *

The allied reprisal fleet came out of space well outside the asteroid belt concealing Hell's Heart. First *MacBeth*, and then more battleships, more cruisers, more destroyers, more frigates, more corvettes, more carriers, and more and more emerge. Duke Ireton, on the bridge of *MacBeth*, looked on as the many starships that came to his aide now fall in about his flagship.

"This is the Lord Admiral", Ireton said. "Commence operation."

Several corvettes broke formation and sped ahead, dispersing around the belt. They linked up with Baden-Powell, still concealed within, and created a real-time system map with a constantly-updated situation report. This included the location of Lord Roland, Countess Gabriela, and Roland's page Creton inside the fortress.

"I see that Lord Roland's plan proceeds as I have foreseen", Old Ireton said.

Captain Denton chuckled. "At least they will be distracted when they do detect our approach."

"Attention all commands." Old Ireton said. "Advance to your staging location and await further orders." The massive fleet now split up into smaller units, dispersing outside the belt to rendezvous with one of the corvettes holding position. Carriers and other ships with mecha aboard prepared to launch, scrambling their pilots and powering up while launch mechanisms got into place. Gunnery crews ran to their positions, reloading crews moving the first volley of missiles into launchers, bulkheads locking down, battle lighting coming on, and the wiser crews getting into vacuum suits."

"Time to knock on the door, Jerry", Old Ireton said. "All ships, launch missiles!"

A thousand vessels around the belt launched missiles that flew into the belt, targeting the mined asteroids, and detonating to fantastic effect.

"It worked very well before", Ireton said. "I'm certain no one will object."

Anti-matter warheads annihilated kilometers of asteroids, blowing holes into the belt's density of floating rock, and this set off alarms inside Hell's Heart. Klaxons sounded throughout the fortress, sending pirate running to their battle stations. Pilots rushed out of wherever they were and ran for their Goblins, crewmen ran for the dock and clambered aboard their ships, gunnery crews climbed into their stations, and fire crews mustered to their assembly points.

"They've come." Red Eyes said, standing in his full uniform in the Grand Hall "We must make this happen now."

Azazel stood ready to receive Gabriela as the groom, inhumanly handsome in his presentation. "No need to worry, High Admiral. The hyperdrives are already online and have begun charging. We can, and should, proceed."

"That's good to know. What I would like to know is what is keeping my sister from bringing the bride to her wedding."

"Whatever the difficulty is, we can presume that this attack will only make it worse."

Red Eyes looked over to the assembled guards. "Go find my sister. Bail her out of whatever mess she's gotten herself into, and them bring the Countess here. If you see Jack while you're out there, get him in here also. It's time to see this matter concluded."

"Aye!" they said and left.

* * *

As the Ireton reprisal fleet gathered over New Edinburgh, Count Vikuun Qis sat in his office in his Oslo house. On his desk, a window opened showing a servant in a mask, one of the many anonymous functionaries back at the Court of Stars in Rome.

"My lord Qis." he said, "What is the purpose for your call?"

"I wish to address the Court regarding the assassination attempt upon me." Qis said.

"A moment."

The screen switched to the heraldry of the Court for a moment before the masked man returned. "My lord, the Speaker agrees to your request. You shall be on presently. Be ready, my lord."

"Very well", Qis said. He waited a few minutes as the Speaker finished announcing the upcoming agenda.

"Now, my lords, Count Vikuun Qis wishes to speak regarding his assassination attempt."

Qis saw an icon on the screen go from red to green, indicating that he was live. "My lords, I have news regarding the assassination attempt upon my life."

Qis brought up a report from the Oslo hospital. "The attempt that took the life of an innocent page serving in my house, the attempt aimed at me, was one that originated in the foul heart of the very pirate warlord that attacked His Grace, Duke Ireton. One of his spies attempted to poison me."

"Now my good uncle prepares to march again in lawful reprisal for the raid upon New Edinburgh and the abduction of my noble cousin, the Countess Gabriela Robin."

"This report shows that the culprit, who took his own life once confronted rather than be captured, bore the brand of the Red Eyes Pirates. He had in his blood a set of chemicals commonplace in those pirates, drugs meant to enhance his performance, and in addition to those drugs the residue of the poison he used appeared on his corpse and in his lair."

"This assassination attempt was put into motion before my return from New Edinburgh, demonstrating that this pirate warlord indeed thinks far beyond the limits of most pirates. If he had succeeded, I would never have made my petition and thus any reprisal would be too weak to succeed."

The Speaker broke in. "What does my lord propose?"

"That we amend the petition to the Holy Father, that we ask him to be declared Anathema, and therefore that Exterminatus be authorized. This warlord is a far greater threat than we had cause to believe previously. We should amend our remedy to address the matter as we know it to be now and inform House Ireton accordingly once we have the Holy Father's declaration."

"The question is before us. Please respond now."

One by one, the lights of the Court's members turned from yellow to green. As before, no one objected. A few minutes later the result was, again, a unanimous agreement to the proposal.

"The proposal passes. The petition shall be amended as directed."

They clean up the mess for me. Fools. Qis thought.

* * *

Ramsey sneaked his way into the Manufacturing Wing of Hell's Heart. The noise of a factory, armory and dockyard combined easily concealed the noise of his approach. He kept to side passages and overhanging gantries to minimize the odds of encountering patrolling pirates.

Those he encountered he cut down quick and hid in nearby niches or tossed over the side down into a vat of molten metal. He made a note of the mecha assembly line, now putting Hobgoblins instead of Goblins, and he saw a second line getting ready for a humanoid line like the one he fought on New Edinburgh.

He saw several ships being refit or repaired, and in a drydock berth he saw what he thought was a new ship being laid down. What made him stop in his tracks was when he turned a corner and caught sight of Minotaur being reassembled.

"Mother of God!" Ramsey said. "That must be the thing that destroyed the previous fleet."

Then he heard an alert in his viewscreen, telling him that Duke Ireton's reprisal fleet had come into the system. He sighed, and put Creton and Gabriela's signals on his screen, knowing that he's got to get moving. He passed through the wing, passed right across Minotaur, and reached the doors into the main hallway of Hell's Heart. On the map he saw Gabriela going to the Grand Hall, while Creton remained in the brig.

Then the klaxons sounded, and the activity shifted. Pirates broke away from all the unessential locations towards a Goblin, to a ship in dock, or somewhere else. Ramsey took a glance down to see if anyone came to get into Minotaur, and no one did.

Knowing that the battle without would clear out most pirates inside, he ducked out of sight for a moment and kept an eye on the tracking signals. Gabriela and Creton started moving apart, and Ramsey moved to intercept Gabriela when he heard a second alarm sound, this time for the Brig.

Quickly running through the possibilities, Ramsey realized what had happened and knew that now both were in mortal danger, especially Creton. All pretense of stealth now abandoned, he rushed every pirate he saw. Those he didn't shoot dead with his pistol fell to his beam sword. As he reached the secure doors that set the Brig from the main hallway, he saw that he had to drop down.

Without a second thought, Ramsey threw himself over the side of the gangway and landed in a three-point stance, catching the pirates responding to the alert by surprise.

"Have at you!" he bellowed, igniting his sword as he stood up. In a few swings he cut down the handful of men there. Then he ran into the Brig, surprising the men manning the checkpoint as they were focused inward and cleared those reavers out with a few blaster bolts. From within he heard screaming between fusillades of furious fire.

"Roland!"

* * *

Gabriela twirled about displaying the golden dress. "Does this satisfy you?"

"I don't care", Zuzu said. "Though I think that the men will find it to their liking."

Now Creton roused, taking the sheet off his face.

"Come on then", Zuzu said, "your husband's waiting."

Creton sat up. "What's going on?"

"Silence, boy. We'll fetch you when we're ready", Zuzu said. She snapped her fingers. Her toady made a quick exit, and three rough-looking men entered the cell.

Creton looked up and saw Gabriela in the white dress. "Are they making you-"

One of the men slapped Creton. "Shut up! She's getting what she's here for, and after she's done, we'll do you up."

Gabriela hesitated as two of the men seized her, each taking an arm. "Creton, please!"

Creton saw the man before him had a pistol tucked into his belt. The pain in his limbs and chest now felt white-hot to him. The heat gave way to something else, something primal, something other than an injured boy. His face seemed to distort as the the rage of his bloodline fell over him, and he struck out in a smooth, swift motion.

He gripped the bed as a brace and kicked up with both feet, catching the pirate square in the chin. As the man snapped back, the boy snatched the pistol out of the man's belt and shot him five times rapid before the man hit the floor stone dead.

"Creton! No!"

"Get her out of here", Zuzu said.

Creton, now possessed by rage, shot down one of the men grabbing Gabriela as he rushed the man. The other, in fear as much as obedience, quit the room pulling Gabriela behind her. Zuzu followed, watching Creton run upon the man he shot and taking that man's pistol. He turned his eyes up, seeing Gabriela being pulled away, and let cry a primal scream as he ran into the hallway both blasters blazing.

"Move!" Zuzu said. She slammed the alarm button and drew her own pistol upon the boy while other guards surged forward to engage. The firefight filled the hall, cutting down a few guards caught out of position, and Zuzu grabbed one of them to use as a shield until she got back around the corner.

Gabriela looked back over her shoulder. "Creton! Stop! This won't help me!"

"He can't hear you, hussy!" Zuzu said as she blind-fired around the corner. "He's somewhere else and he ain't coming back."

A wave of dread washed over Gabriela as Zuzu's men pulled her farther and farther away from Creton. The boy slowly gained ground, throwing one drained pistol and then the other before picking up replacements and resuming fire.

Then Gabriela turned to see Ramsey before her, ready for action.

"Roland!"

* * *

The volleys of missiles flew into the belt, one after the next. Anti-matter warheads annihilated whole swathes of floating rock, disintegrating the labyrinth surrounding Hells' Heart that shielded it from direct assault.

Meanwhile, the gunnery crews of Hell's Heart got to their positions. They traced the missile trajectories back, estimating where beyond their sensor range the ships likely lead.

A first volley of counter-missiles launched, and the crews tracked them closely. As soon as the fleet's point-defense weapons shot the missiles down the pirate gunners marked the coordinates and launched a larger volley, with nuclear warheads, at those locations.

Aboard the flagship *MacBeth*, the Communications Officer alerted Duke Ireton: "My Lord Admiral, the New Romans report that the pirates have nuclear warheads mixed into their missile barrages."

"Navigation, asteroid density."

"Reduced by over 50%, Lord Admiral."

"Jerry?"

Captain Gerald Denton, standing beside Ireton, knew the question: "Do you think we're ready to move in?" He gave his answer, "Time to square up."

"All commands, this is the Lord Admiral. Advance and engage the fortress. Launch all mecha."

Across the fleet, squadrons of mecha launched from their motherships. At the same time, streams of Goblins launched out of the docking bay of Hell's Heart and from the carriers moored outside.

Smaller pirate vessels, their crews now aboard and their captains ready, raised anchor and sailed out of the docks. Only *Redalen's Revenge* remained now, with its captain and its executive abandoning everything else to rush to get aboard and get her out into the fight.

"He'll be mad that you quit the ceremony for this", Gori said as they ran.

"He'd be mad if I didn't", Jack said. "He'll forgive us both if we somehow get a win out of this."

Jack keyed into his ship's command coms. "This is the Captain. We're coming out hot. I want the Hobgoblins ready to launch when I give the command, and I want *Black Knight* ready for when I arrive."

"Battle plan?" Gori said.

"Those carriers need to run, so we need to buy time", Jack said. "We'll take Revenge, get as many of the smaller ships as we can, and sally out to the weakest of their units. We bust a hole in the line. We can get the carriers out that way and they can jump to the rendezvous point."

"Aye, Captain. And you?"

"Until someone brings out *Minotaur*, I will lead our mecha units as best I can."

Gori and Jack saw *Revenge* waiting for her, engines revving, and made for her ramp.

"I've got a bad feeling about this." Gori said.

"Roland hasn't shown his face, has he?"

"Or he's here, but we can't deal with him because of this mess."

They ran up the ramp, which retracted as they ran up its length. The hatch sealed right behind them once aboard and they felt the ship shudder as its engines went to full power.

"Gori, jump if you get into trouble," Jack said as he made for *Revenge*'s flight deck." Don't worry about me. I have my ace up my sleeve."

"Aye!" Gori said as he got into the lift towards the bridge.

* * *

A toady ran into the Grand Hall. "High Admiral, they're here!"

Red Eyes shot the toady dead. "I have no time for fools telling me what I already know." Then he turned to Azazel. "I'm afraid you're going to have to wait a little longer, my friend."

"It would help if your sister would drag the girl here."

Red Eyes called over another toady, this one rolling a holographic projector over, and turned it on. It displayed a battlemap of the space about Hell's Heart, showing the fleet's attempt to englobe the fortress. "They cannot be serious."

"They are. Look at how they're systematically reducing the asteroid density before advancing into gunnery range. They're launching their mecha now to screen out our Goblins, hoping to get a chance to target our exposed subsystems once they somehow break our pilots. The carriers are already looking to withdraw but cannot escape."

"I see *Revenge* is on its way out. Well played, Jack. You forced the ceremony's delay."

"Let him. He's more useful out there now."

Red Eyes sighed. "Mice, men, and plans", he said. He sifted through the windows to find Zuzu. He came upon the Brig's feed, where he saw Zuzu being put upon by a berserk Creton, and he laughed for a moment before the camera shifted to reveal Ramsey's ambush on the rear of Zuzu's group and his liberation of Gabriela. Now what mirth Red Eyes felt fell away, and Azazel put a hand on the warlord's shoulder.

"Until she's mine, she's your problem. Handle it. I'll go ready *Minotaur*. Tell your sister that *Anakim* is ready for her in the meantime", Azazel said.

The angel turned his back on Red Eyes and walked out of the Grand Hall by a side entrance, ignoring the ongoing chaos as he returned to his workshop in the Manufacturing Wing, and leaving the pirate warlord to deal with the infiltration and rescue without angelic aid.

"Fine, angel." Red Eyes stalked his way towards the main doors to the Grand Hall. "Then handle it I shall."

Red Eyes considered which issue to handle first. The fleet had to be handled, but Jack was already there and certainly would not bother trying without a plan of his own. Let the Jack sort that front out, Red Eyes thought. The ceremony is moot so long as there is a real threat of disruption or prevention, so that could be shunted aside.

That left Countess Gabriela Robin. That meant going to the Brig. That meant backing up his sister. That meant recovering the prize from Lord Roland, and that meant a face-to-face fight against one of the elite warriors of Christendom, and that meant the opportunity to score a glorious victory that ignited a fire in his heart he could not deny.

* * *

Gabriela embraced Ramsey. "You've come! Thank God!"

He returned her embrace. "I'm here for you, and Creton."

Gabriela turned to look back into the Brig. "He's gone berserk. Seeing me like this incited him, and he's beyond reason."

Inside, the screaming continued as Creton ran around the corner with both blasters blazing. One, two, three, four, all stunned at this berserk boy's violence of action, and that error got them killed by blaster fire to their faces. Only Zuzu survived, again, by taking one of them and using him as a shield from which she fired back. She kept her cool, letting Creton close, keeping up the corpse shield to soak that blaster fire. Once he got into range, Zuzu threw the corpse at him, knowing he'd dodge it and that no matter which way he went he'd be within reach of her arms.

"Roland", Gabriela said, "please."

Ramsey knew her mind, and he meant to go rescue the boy, but just then he heard the words that held him fast: "Stand and deliver!"

Gabriela moved behind Ramsey, who pivoted to face Red Eyes. He saw Red Eyes standing half again his height, skin slick with sweat making his royal blue skin gleam in the light, and his massive mane of blood-red hair loose and flowing free. They squared up. She knew he couldn't deal with this and save Creton, and she felt a grip about her heart as she looked first at Red Eyes stalking towards she and Ramsey like a ravenous tiger, then over to Creton now grappling with Zuzu: an adult giantess over three times his height and twice his weight. Something had to be done.

No, that she had to do something, something here, something now, something she never thought she would never do.

"I want to live on", she said, faintly, still holding on to Ramsey.

Ramsey caught the tone in her voice. He kept his gaze on Red Eyes, who now drew his beam sword and ignited it. The red beam seemed to manifest out of the rage in the pirate's heart. Ramsey answered by swapping his own sword to his main hand and igniting it, presenting a golden blade to face Red Eyes's own.

"I want to live on!" she said, and she looked at Creton screaming as he squirmed in Zuzu's grasp. He faced Zuzu and bit her nose, drawing blood and making the giantess howl in a pain that also turned into rage and threw a surge of strength into her limbs.

In a moment, Gabriela seized Ramsey's pistol out of his hand. As she did, she leaned into him and said, "I love you."

Ramsey didn't contest, but he felt a bit of worry. As Gabriela rushed to Creton's aid, Red Eyes smiled. "That suits me fine, Lord Roland. Nothing to save you, nothing to stop me, nothing will keep me from taking your head!"

Gabriela got clear of Ramsey as Red Eyes rushed him. She got to the doorway to the Brig, where she stopped and leveled the pistol at Zuzu. She hesitated, remembering what her father taught her, beating away the grip of fear about her heart by taking control of her breathing and focusing on the giantess. She saw Zuzu struggling to stay on her feet, Creton trying to throw his weight around in order to get Zuzu to fall over, and soon she got her chance. Zuzu had to turn her back to Gabriela, unaware that the woman had a pistol in hand, and thus got taken by surprise when Gabriela shot her in the back. She shot Zuzu once, twice, thrice before Zuzu dropped Creton to the floor and ran around the corner.

"Creton!" Gabriela said. "Come to me! Come, now!"

Red Eyes's rush came at Ramsey like a charging bull, but one light on his feet. Ramsey tried to sidestep the rush, but instead Red Eyes adjusted his line and met the knight in a clash of blades. Gabriela now ran out of the Brig with

Creton, the boy coming down from the rage, and before she could try to shoot Red Eyes Creton took the blaster from her.

"Never try that", Creton said. "You're as likely to shoot him as you would Red Eyes."

Then Creton collapsed into Gabriela, exhausted. She scooped him up, thrust the pistol into the sash at her waist, and look at Ramsey.

"What now?" Gabreila said.

"There's a beacon! Follow the signal to it and call for Sibley." Ramsey yelled, "I'll hold him here. Get out now!

10 A FOOLHARDY RESCUE

Sibley saw the signals for Creton and Gabriela heading for the airlock Ramsey used to get into Hell's Heart. He powered up *Baden-Powell*, heated up the turret's guns, disengaged the clamp hold the ship to the asteroid, and engaged the engines.

"*Baden-Powell* to *MacBeth*", Sibley said. "Recovering the Countess. Requesting support."

"Acknowledged, *Baden-Powell*." Ireton turned to Captain Denton, who turned to the Navigation Officer.

"Lega Roma's Knights of the Eagle are closest." Navigation said, "They're closing on the enemy battleship."

"Lega Roma, this is the Lord Admiral. Lord Roland's ship is on approach to recover the objective. Cover *Baden-Powell*."

A dozen gleaming silver Cataphracts, scintillating counterparts to Dashing Jack's *Black Knight*, changed course from intercepting *Redalen's Revenge* to form up around Baden-Powell.

"Gentlemen, I shall not keep you from your vendetta for long", Sibley said.

Goblins came at them in a disorganized mass, swarm-firing missiles at their formation. Counter-fire from Baden-Powell and the Eagle Knights' Cataphracts cleared away most of them, and then they fired upon the Goblins just as the pirates got into range with their own guns. Blaster bolts deflected off *Baden-Powell*'s shields, which the Roma pilots exploited to minimize their exposure until it was too late for the pirates.

Fanning out at the last moment, beam rifles blazing, the first wave got blown apart without mercy. The second wave attempted to change their approach to maintain some distance, but the pirates' inferior discipline, skill, and quality of machines told quickly. The Eagle Knights sensed that their adversaries got shaken, and in that window they closed and blasted that second wave apart at point-blank range; the last thing several pilots saw was the barrel of a Cataphract beam rifle swallowing their field of view before firing the fatal shot.

Sibley didn't slack off. He let the tri-barrelled beam cannon turret launch lethal light lances, each barrel tracking a separate target before firing, destroying three Goblins per volley.

With this many so close a larger vessel had to be nearby, Sibley thought. Soon he detected one of the pirate's carriers, and as his escort cleaned up the enemy mecha he took aim at its engines and unleashed vollies at them while steering clear of the carrier's point defense cannons. A few volleys did the job, sending the engine compartment up into a bilious fireball that consumed the whole ship.

"We're almost there. Make a defense line around the ship", Sibley said.

The Cataphracts surged forward, clearing out the Goblins nearby, while Sibley identified the point-defense cannons and fired upon them. One after the next went up, blowing out chucks of rock along with the destroyed cannon and its crew, until all the cannons covering the airlock became smoking craters.

"*Baden-Powell*, the way is clear." The squadron leader said as he pulled alongside the ship. "We'll hold here until you're away."

"Acknowledged." Sibley said, and he flew up to the airlock. Landing on the surface of Hell's Heart, he extended the ventral hatch as he would if boarding a ship. Then he went down the hatch and opened the airlock. Gabriela stood there waiting, holding an exhausted Creton in her arms.

"Quickly, my lady!" Sibley said, taking Gabriela by her free hand and hurrying her aboard Baden-Powell.

"*Baden-Powell*", an Eagle Knight said. "We have an enemy unit fast approaching."

Sibley disengaged the ventral hatch and fired up the ship's engines again.

"It's the enemy's other ace unit." Sibley said, "Be careful."

"Acknowledged, *Baden-Powell*", the Eagle Knight Commander said., "We'll drive them away from you."

The Cataphracts fired upon *Anakim*, forcing Zuzu to deal with them.

"You want to interfere? Then you shall die right here!" she said, growling at them as she opened fire. However, her own lack of discipline and composure soon had her on the backfoot. They took turns coming, engaging her, pushing her away from *Baden-Powell*, and disengaging while the next man moved in. Using their superior skill, discipline, and numbers they easily countered her attacks and maneuvered her towards their objective: *Redalen's Revenge*.

Baden-Powell took advantage of the distraction and move at full speed for the rear, where *MacBeth* would be.

"*Baden-Powell* to *MacBeth*", Sibley said. "I have the Countess. Coming to your location."

"Acknowledged, *Baden-Powell*", Old Ireton said. "Attention all commands. We have the Countess."

Zuzu growled as she raged against her seeming impotence against the Cataphract squadron, knowing that they weren't seeking to outright kill her so much as they aimed to fatigue her while driving her towards her comrade's battleship.

"Zuzu!" Gori said, "Withdraw to *Revenge*'s hangar bay. The captain's coming to relieve you."

Just then she saw the sensors detect *Black Knight* and *Revenge*'s Hobgoblin squadron formed up behind him. As they opened fire on the Cataphracts, relieving her, she turned and withdrew, making straight for the hangar bay as Gori told her.

"Gori!" she said. "I want *Anakim* rearmed and topped off when I come in."

"Hangar Bay, you heard the Vice Admiral", Gori said, monitoring the battle. "Captain, I'm executing the plan now. Be careful out there."

* * *

Red Eyes took full advantage of his massive advantage in height and weight over Ramsey, exploiting his reach to seize control of his duel with the Star Knight.

His face became a mask of wrath, like the demons of old. He broke the clench, and now estimating just how much stronger he was over Ramsey he stopped holding back.

The next blow he struck, he knew Ramsey would block instead of dodge. The force of the blow sent Ramsey sprawling down and across the hall, ending with him slamming into the far wall. Red Eyes, pleased with the result, let his smile become a toothy wide smirk as he felt a predator's presumption of victory over his prey fill him.

Ramsey, shocked at the force and ferocity, scrambled back to his feet. He realized that Red Eyes had cut himself loose. Ramsey now faced the full power and prowess of the pirate warlord.

Red Eyes bellowed a great roar and charged at Ramsey. Ramsey saw Red Eyes draw the blade high as the pirate charged at him. Ramsey dodged at the last moment, going against the stroke and just under it, seeing that rigid red beam blade goes just over his head and gouge deep into the wall.

He counter-attacked, his own reach just enough to clip Red Eyes' ribcage, provoking a great howl of pain followed by a blind stroke in his direction, one he easily dodged.

"You're a beast, Red Eyes, and beasts are easily taken once they're measured", Ramsey said.

Red Eyes took a step back and stood once more to his full height. "Bold words." Red Eyes pointed his sword at Ramsey. "You're not unskilled if you can tag me with that toy."

"I can tell", Ramsey said as the two began circling each other, "you're not used to fighting men who can challenge you."

"It's far too rare." Red Eyes watched Ramsey's hands, seeing him change his stance. "But I know I can still take your head."

Ramsey tested Red Eyes, jabbing at him, feinting left, then right, probing the pirate's defenses. Red Eyes kept his stance closed, not letting Ramsey get inside his reach, and keeping his gaze fixed where the tells would be.

Ramsey seemed satisfied, which puzzled Red Eyes, but not enough to keep talking. Instead he put that puzzlement behind a snarl and came again at Ramsey. Ramsey hustled with his footwork, shifting left, then right, deflecting each blow up and away as he moved to the next spot to block the next attack.

Red Eyes saw the scheme, that Ramsey wanted to tire Red Eyes before committing to an attack and began pushing Ramsey down the hall and then into the hangar bays where the mecha yet to be launched awaited. At this time Red Eyes saw Zuzu pass them, running for *Anakim*, and Red Eyes then glanced up at the alarm of another hostile ship coming.

"Is that yours?" Red Eyes said.

"It is", Ramsey said.

"Aren't you going to-"

"No."

Then it became clear to Red Eyes what Ramsey's plan was: hold him here until the Countess got away, then break off and escape himself as soon as he could thereafter. "You expect to escape, don't you?"

"Maybe."

"Don't tell me that you're willing to die for her", Red Eyes chuckled. "Sure, she's a rare prize, but there isn't a treasure so great I'd be ready to die for it."

"That's why you will lose."

"Let's see how you feel after you're dead!"

Ramsey knew Red Eyes meant to charge for him again, maybe this time to grapple and go body-to-body, and Ramsey saw that this too was a good time to play at delaying.

As soon as Red Eyes rushed at him, Ramsey slipped to one side and moved the fight. Red Eyes followed by making a great leap, clearing a pile of parts taller than him, intending to crash down blade-first upon Ramsey, but Ramsey wasn't there.

Red Eyes was off by just a few paces, and Ramsey punished the error with a cut at Red's head. Instead, Ramsey sliced off Red's massive blood-red mane of hair leaving a clean-cut ending at the pirate's neck, and then quickly stepped back out of reach.

Red Eyes saw the pile of hair fall about him, reached back with his off-hand, realized what Ramsey had done, and laughed. "Oh, ho. I will savor this kill. You're making me work for it."

Now Ramsey surprised Red Eyes again, cutting a cable holding up a cargo net. It dropped down on Red Eyes, who started cutting at it before it covered him, but not before it gave Ramsey an opportunity to attack him in passing as he maneuvered again to move the fight. Red saw the golden blade's line of attack and batted it away, but that was still enough effort to keep from counter-attacking before getting free of the netting.

Red Eyes followed Ramsey, again leaping into the air, this time landing just before Ramsey and cutting him off.

"If that was your escape plan, you're more a fool that I thought."

"No."

"Then how, exactly, were you intending to escape?"

"I'm going to walk out of here on my own two feet", Ramsey said. "I don't need anything else."

Red Eyes threw back his head to laugh at Ramsey, laughing loud enough to fill the hangar bay. "You magnificent, arrogant, naive fool! I shall sing a song of your futile valor for years after I mount your head on the wall."

Ramsey taunting the pirate. "If you can take it."

"I will", Red Eyes said. "Because you're trapped here. Sooner or later your guard slips, and when it does you will die."

* * *

Gori, on the bridge of *Redalen's Revenge*, noticed all the allied fleet advancing. "They're coming in!" he said. "Goblins cover your carriers, escorts with *Revenge*."

The battleship formed up with a dozen cruisers, corvettes, and destroyers. Accelerating to full speed, they assumed an arrowhead formation with *Revenge* at the tip and moved to the weakest of the allied elements, a squadron of about the same composition from New Praetoria in Boer Space.

"Corvettes, counter-fire and intercept their mecha. Frigates, destroyers, follow Revenge's lead." Gori said. The New Praetorians launched missiles and send their mecha forward. Gori's corvettes kept both machines and missiles away from Revenge, while the battleship counter-launched a volley. The others followed, creating a one-two punch effect. The first punch got shot down, but the second got through and took out a few escorts near the New Praetorian flagship.

"Peel the onion and do it fast!" Gori said. The Weapons Officer passed target designations to the gunners in the turrets, who each took a different ship near the battleship while the escorts aimed for the outside wings of the New Praetorian formation. Missiles again flew between the formations, most of which got shot down by the point-defense cannons, but enough got through and sank a New Praetorian frigate.

The Weapons Officer gave the countdown to the main contest: "Guns in range in three seconds, two, one."

"FIRE!" Gori bellowed with a deep-throated yalp. The turreted primary cannons on *Revenge* exploded as they launched their blue-white beams across the short space between the formations. Each of the nine shots raced towards its target and lanced one of the ships escorting the flagship, sinking it, and then the shot continued to hit the flagship's shields. In an instant, the escort screen for the New Praetorian formation had a battleship-sized hole blown out of it.

The escorts each fired to the outside of the formation, each one also sinking another ship, and suddenly half of the enemy formation was gone. New Praetorian return fire sank a frigate that trailed in Gori's formation, and a corvette went down once it too fell out of formation, but those losses did nothing to Gori's demeanor or focus.

"Come about and do it again!" Gori said, "Rip those Boer wings right off!"

The New Praetorians immediately turned to face Gori and his squadron, maintaining gun fire that clipped a second corvette and first knocked it out of formation before a second volley blew it apart in a spectacular fireball. Yet another exchange of missiles followed, stressing Gori and his escorts more now that two corvettes weren't there to do most of the anti-missile work, but still not scoring any hits yet. The same result happened for the New Praetorians, a small mercy in a moment of madness, but it was all too brief.

"Fire!" Gori said. Once more the turrets of *Revenge's* guns blasted at the formation's remnants and dealt death in deft blows, slicing off the remaining wing from its flagship while the escorts finished the job. Returning fire caught a destroyer and the last two corvettes, but now it was battleship to battleship for all intents and purposes, and Gori knew that this was a one-on-one he and *Revenge* could win

"The rest of you turn back and resume escorting the carriers out. Revenge can finish this job on its own."

As the pirate formation turned for a final pass, the escorts remaining peeled off and headed back to the carriers. *Revenge* continued alone, coming at the Boer battleship with all guns blazing. The Boers returned fire, and the two ships pummeled each other with neither grace nor mercy. Shields scintillated as generators took all they could before overloading and either shorting out or exploding, but Gori got the measure of the Boers first. He fired specifically to overload the shields on a given spot, and as *Revenge* passed he made clear what that meant.

The rear turret turned and fired into the hole in the shields, a tri-barrel volley flying across a gap small enough to throw a rock and striking the Boer battleship one-two-three across the hull near the aft where the engines were. The shots burned through the armor, just so, and touched off a fuel line. The explosion cascaded quickly, going to the engines and the thrusters, and then the battleship's hull blistered from within before erupting in a series of explosive plumes. Finally, the few missiles remaining went off and finished the job, ripping the crippled battleship apart and killing anyone left who had hoped to escape the ship's destruction.

Revenge returned to the fleet. "Mission accomplished." Gori said, "Mark my location and send the carriers out this way."

"Good job, Gori!" Jack said, "Losses?"

"Not many, but still too much. What's your situation?"

"Not good, Gori. The sooner you can get back here, the better we'll be. If it weren't for Zuzu and I, we wouldn't have any carriers to escort out of here."

* * *

Zuzu launched from the hangar bay of *Revenge* as the battleship moved to find a weak point in the allied formation and secure an escape route for the carriers. *Anakim* now carried an arsenal of weapons, and she immediately moved to support Dashing Jack.

"How many on you?"

"Nevermind me", Jack said as he sidestepped and struck down a Cataphract with a beam sword. "I'm holding fine for now. Get their mothership."

Zuzu cycled through the ship signatures on *Anakim*'s sensors until she found the New Roman League's ships. "On it!"

Anakim's engines spun up to top speed and shot off like a rocket. Zuzu dodged one rock after the next to mask her approach and confuse enemy gunners. The New Roman League ships sent out alerts, recalling several of the Cataphracts engaged with Jack, but they didn't return fast enough. Soon Zuzu emerged from cover and closed with the New Roman fleet.

"Now you shall see the might of *Anakim*, Roman dogs!" Zuzu declared on open coms. "Watch as I rend your fleet to shreds like the Red Comet!"

Anakim bore a missile launcher on each arm and carried both a beam rifle and a long rifle on its back in addition to rocket pods on its legs. Zuzu locked in multiple targets as she bore down on them, and once she got in close-combat range she let loose. She fired one launcher, then the other, each at separate ships. Too close for the point-defense cannons to track, the missiles quickly hit and they hit near the aft where the thrusters and the engines mated. The explosions ripped apart the ship, blowing it apart and sinking it.

"Two!" Zuzu said as she turned on her axis to fire another missile, which also hit and sunk its target.

"Three!" Zuzu fired again, taking another down, and now the flagship appeared: *Sulla*, the last of the obsolete *Equis*-class battleships. It, and the handful of frigates and corvettes escorting it, erupted as its point-defense cannons attempted to track and shoot down *Anakim*.

"You think that rustbucket can stop me?" Zuzu launched missiles at the escorts as she closed, firing into the blindsides of their defense cannons and destroying them one after the next. *Sulla*'s gunners tried to track *Anakim*, but the mecha's speed and agility confounded them, allowing Zuzu to finish off her escorts. She put away one of the launchers, swapping for the beam rifle, as she saw the battleship's hangar bay still open. Knowing that the closing doors would not close fast enough, she slipped into *Sulla*'s bay and opened fire.

She hovered about the bay, quickly identifying explosive targets such as fuel and munitions, and blasting it apart. The explosions ruptured the blast doors, making them weak enough to fire through, which Zuzu did. A few more such shots told with a massive backblast; she hit one of the missile tubes going to a launcher, and now the magazine went up. Knowing that she had certainly crippled Sulla, she blasted the door down and flew back into space to finish the job by blasting into the thrusters in the rear. One proximity warning later and she cleared the area just as the battleship finished its cascade of explosions, hitting the engines, blowing it apart and sinking Sulla.

"Now to finish this wretched fleet off!" Zuzu said, swapping the beam rifle for the long rifle, and she began lobbing railgun slugs through the armored hulls of the escorts remaining. She saw a flight of Cataphracts finally catching up to her and laughed.

"Too late, dogs! Your master's gone to meet his God!"

Zuzu erupted into a bout of maniacal laughter as she closed with, shot into, and sank the final ship, a fleeing corvette. Now the Cataphracts got her full attention and she swapped the long rifle for her beam rifle again. She closed with them at the same speed she closed with the ships, catching the pilots off-guard as she did the crews, and once she knew she approached close-combat range she hit them with the leg-mounted rockets. Three moved out of the way, but the man up front was too close to act in time and took the full volley. He exploded in an instant, shooting him down. The other three chased *Anakim*, firing upon him with beam rifles, but got caught out when Zuzu flung *Anakim* in a 180 reverse and fired back. Again, the leader of the three was too close to react in time; the first shot hit square, and the follow-ups got through the armor, penetrating the cockpit and blowing up the powerplant.

"Two left." Zuzu said as she saw them split up. She saw them circle about, seeking to cover each other; one engages and the other covers, then switch off. She drew the long rifle, marked both as targets to track and lock on. Once both targets locked, she fired. She caught one of them with the beam rifle, tagging it in the back and setting off the powerplant. The other took a slug the long way, going in through the head servo, through the torso, down a leg, and out a foot. Both exploded, and once more Zuzu erupted in triumphant maniacal laughter as she sped away from the wreckage she wrought.

"That did it!" she said over the coms. "Jack, what's your situation?"

"You got the rookies." Jack said, "Their aces are on me, and we're getting pressed in here."

Zuzu locked in Jack's location and set her course. "I'm on my way."

Zuzu resumed her high-speed transit through the battlefield, taking the time now to reload the launchers and the long rifle. Already one of the carriers got sunk, and another now went up under missile barrages from very long range overwhelming its point-defense cannons and nearby Goblin screen.

* * *

Ramsey saw on his helmet visor the ongoing situation of the battle outside. Red Eyes had a running audio feed going into one ear.

"You have to know", Ramsey said, "that you're being pressed on all sides outside. Two, no three sunk carriers. Several corvettes, destroyers, and frigates now sunk also, and let's not talk about the casualties your mecha force has taken so far."

"And your alliance has had two of its members wiped out to a man, forcing your fleet to close in and spread thin at the same time. That puts your fleet into range of my guns, and that means your fleet has to contend both with my fortress as well as my fleet."

"Who is trapped with whom, then? I've rescued the Countess. My allies will reduce this fortress to rubble. It's unlikely that you'll escape alive, and if you do it won't be with the forces you've had until now."

Red Eyes answered with a renewed attack, now having full measure of his reach advantage over Ramsey. His strikes now kept Ramsey within that meter or so of space that he had over his foe, allowing only blocks from Ramsey.

"Do you see this, fool?" he said, driving Ramsey back and back. "I have you. I've got your measurement now. You won't escape me, you're not fast enough. You can't close with me, I've seen the limits of your skill."

Ramsey knew Red Eyes wasn't all talk. The pirate did find a way to fix him into a dead zone where the pirate could reach him, but not vice-versa. But he saw over his visor that this engagement had reached the end of its usefulness.

He saw that while he's been fixed into a dead zone he had control over where to move this fight, so he moved it back, and then up several flights of stairs leading to a walkway running even with the massive chest of *Minotaur*. With everything else deployed, the hangars now stood empty. The walkway meant for someone to reach *Minotaur*'s cockpit from the floor also meant that it high up enough to make a fall lethal.

"You're good, Red Eyes", Ramsey said. "That is the truth, sure enough, but you're not as good as you think you are." Ramsey blocked another strike, this time directing it down to cut into the railing.

"Bold words from a man barely keeping his guard up." Red Eyes fixed his gaze on the man, unthinking that he's cutting into and severing segments of the walkway's railing when Ramsey blocks his blows.

"You think yourself some genius warlord, but you forgot the most important duty a commanding officer must fulfill", Ramsey said, positioning himself at the cross point of a T-section.

"My men are capable", Red Eyes said, slicing through one more railing. "They know the plan, and they can handle changes as they occur."

Ramsey blocked another blow, forcing Red Eyes to slice through and sever the railing behind him, leaving Ramsey nowhere to go as Red Eyes closed to his optimum distance.

"You still don't see it, do you?" Ramsey smiled at him, and Red Eyes got a sense that Ramsey implied knowing something that he didn't. Red Eyes heard over his comlink that his subordinates outside had opened an escape route for the carriers, but Jack had become hard pressed by the New Roman ace mecha pilots and Zuzu had run low on munitions. The escorts couldn't leave their position with the carriers, and his mecha force had been getting pounded severely.

Ramsey watched Red Eyes' face, seeing in the pirate's eyes that his words struck their mark and compelled the pirate to consider the situation. In his visor, he saw that the fleet's main battle line had come into optimum range. Now the missiles again swarmed from the fleet, this time targeting Hell's Heart directly, and with those volleys came bombardment by the guns, scores of guns, each capable of scrapping a lesser ship in a single shot. Ramsey guessed that Red Eyes now got reports from his gunners of the main battleships being in range and firing upon the fortress.

Red Eyes realized now the full extent of Ramsey's gambit. It wasn't merely to buy time for his man and his page to escape with Gabriela, but to buy time for the full fleet to begin reducing the fortress to rubble. The realization of how thoroughly he'd been played showed on his face, which let Ramsey realize that his reading of Red Eyes was correct.

"You're too short-sighted to win", Ramsey said. "You lost sight of the situation to focus only upon this one part, and now it's too late to prevent your ruin."

Red Eyes, unable to retort, growled at Ramsey as he took a massive overhead blow at the man, but Ramsey saw it coming and leaped off the walkway. With a roll in the air, Ramsey shut off and put away his beam sword. Then in a smooth, practiced motion he drew once more the baton in his boot.

"Roland, *draw your sword*!"

Red Eyes looked on, impotent, and watched the Star Knight summon forth the very mecha that fought *Anakim* and forced Zuzu to withdraw.

"Now watch, Red Eyes", Ramsey said as he settled into the cockpit of *Durendal*. "Watch me show you how good your men really are."

Ramsey revved up the engine and threw open the thrusters as he turned and left the bay, shooting out into space to join his allies out there. Red Eyes extinguished his sword, tucking it back into his belt, and listened as he walked up to *Minotaur*.

"Not yet, Roland." Red Eyes said, "I am not finished yet."

"Hold!" Red Eyes heard Azazel call to him, "We're doing better than expected. They just need to hold that fleet off a little longer and we can jump this fortress out of here."

11 THE BATTLE OF HELL'S HEART

On *Revenge*, Gori took a deep breath at this big change in the battle. Jack recognized the severity of the situation while fending off the four New Roman aces still out to get him, and Zuzu felt a sense of dread at the news.

"Gori!" Zuzu said. "I'm almost dry. I need to come in!"

"Get in if you can and make it fast", Jack said. "You're no good out here with just a sword." More missiles flew in from far away now, coming straight for the fortress. "They're reorganizing their battle line", Gori said. "Battleships, carriers, and heavy cruisers are standing off while their escorts are coming in to assist the mecha. They're going for a partial englobement."

"How many more carriers to go?" Jack said, slipping past the ace flight once more and dodging around a rock.

Gori looked on the viewscreen. "Three sunk. Three away. That leaves four. We're going to be pressed hard to hold this fleet back until everyone else is away."

"We've got our ace in the hole." Zuzu said, now approaching the ventral aft of Revenge as its hangar ramp extended, "He's come out if it gets that bad."

As Zuzu approached the battleship, Ramsey in *Durendal* marked the location of *Anakim*, *Revenge*, and Jack's *Black Knight*, the massive Goblin horde as well as *Revenge*'s Hobgoblin squadron. The remaining pirate escorts and carriers then got marked. Ramsey forwarded that data to *Baden-Powell*, which spread it to the rest of the allied fleet.

"Where's that Solar Guardsman?" Jack said, finally getting one of those aces with a beam sword through the chest and destroying it.

Zuzu, taking in some drinks while the technicians on *Revenge*'s flight deck hurry through rearming, "Gori?"

Gori looked at the viewscreen for a moment. "Oh no!"

Ramsey locked on to Jack's *Black Knight*. "Coming to assist, New Romans." He closed into range for his beam rifle, and quickly fell in for the fallen comrade, needing no time to adjust to the aces' teamwork. Yet, having superior power, it became apparent to the three aces that Ramsey should take the lead and wordlessly let him assume the front position in their flight.

"Skip the launchers!" Gori said, calling down to the bay. "Rockets and the long rifle. GO!"

Zuzu tossed her empties out and closed up the cockpit as the technicians strapped the rocket pods to *Anakim*'s legs. A few more attached spare magazines to *Anakim*'s hips, and Zuzu took the long rifle in hand as she again departed *Revenge*'s hangar.

"I'm on my way!" Zuzu said.

"Good!" Jack said, dodging rifle fire from one direction while in hand-to-hand with another and Ramsey circling for another opening, "I'm also running low and need to fall back."

Anakim's thrusters went to full burn and rocketed Zuzu to Jack's location. As she approached, she took aim with the long rifle and fired. One of the other Cataphracts flew behind a rock, but it wasn't enough. The rifle's slug penetrated the rock and lodged into the doomed pilot's powerplant, causing to explode in a brilliant fireball.

"Stay on *Black Knight*!" Ramsey said. "I'll take care of this one."

Ramsey peeled off, beam rifle ready. Zuzu took aim with the rifle and fired, but Ramsey rolled away from the line of fire with aplomb. Zuzu countered by launching her pods at him, forcing Ramsey to shoot them down and giving Zuzu concealment for her next shot. Ramsey rolled away from that one also, and the next, until he got within range for his rifle. Zuzu swapped to *Anakim*'s beam rifle and the two began darting between rocks and wrecks, attempting to catch the other out of positions for a fatal shot.

Several rocks got blasted to pebbles, and several wrecks got blasted to pieces, as each scored near-hits that would have proven fatal had they come just a moment earlier or later than when they got under cover. Then Zuzu got an opening on Ramsey, but Ramsey rolled off the line and then threw power into the thrusters to rush Zuzu; he swapped the rifle for the beam sword, and Zuzu had to toss her rifle away to get *Anakim*'s out to block in time.

"Not this time!" Ramsey said, grabbing *Anakim*'s main hand arm with his off-hand and shoving *Anakim* into a nearby rock. With his sword arm he reversed the blade and brought it down to thrust into *Anakim*'s neck. Zuzu saw the stroke coming and tried to block the stroke with her off-hand arm, but even with the beam sword's blade going through that arm it was not enough. The beam burned through the off-hand forearm, through-and-through its armor and structure, and then pierced *Anakim* at the neck. Zuzu knew *Anakim* was now doomed and punched out.

"Damn you, Roland!" she yelled as she recovered her bearings. "I'm going in for our trump card. I'm tired of this."

Ramsey didn't hesitate to change targets once he saw Zuzu punch out. He grabbed the long rifle off *Anakim*'s back and took aim at *Black Knight*. "One shot left, but it's all I need."

Ramsey took aim, waited for the other two Cataphracts to get out of the line of fire, and then fired. Jack felt his mecha lurch with the impact, ripping through the back thrusters. That was enough. Unable to maneuver, Jack soon got overwhelmed and had *Black Knight*'s limbs severed one-two, one-two. He too punched out, getting clear just before the New Roman aces finished *Black Knight* off.

"Withdraw to *MacBeth*." Ramsey said to the New Roman aces, "You've gotten your revenge."

"Almost. The battleship remains."

* * *

Red Eyes looked out into the battle outside. "Is *Minotaur* ready."

"Yes", Azazel said. "*Anakim*'s gone, so your sister will be coming for it presently."

Red Eyes keyed into his comlink. "One of you mooks bring in the Vice Admiral."

A Goblin saw Zuzu slowly floating across the battlespace back to Hell's Heart. He withdrew from his position, pulled up alongside Zuzu and waited for her to grab a hold before flying her back into the hangar bay.

The pilot saluted without saying a word and went back into the fight. Zuzu took a moment to collect herself and then scaled the stairs leading to the walkway before *Minotaur*, where she saw Red Eyes standing there.

"The angel says that *Minotaur* is ready, sister." Red Eyes said.

"Orders, High Admiral?"

"Support *Revenge* until the carriers are away. Then find our prize and get her back. You'll have to break their fleet to find her, but we still need her alive so take care."

"Bringing *Minotaur* up", Azazel said as Zuzu entered the massive robot's cockpit. "Vice Admiral, you'll find several additions and upgrades since your last sortie."

Zuzu felt several micro-waldos clamp into her armored suit, each point of attachment then seeming to prick her, but before she could object, she saw this come over her visor: "DNA key accepted. Unlocking unit features."

Now the cockpit revealed itself to be a 360-degree sphere, just like *Anakim*, but with her standing instead of in a cockpit seat.

"*Minotaur* is now a true extension of your body, Vice Admiral." Azazel said, "You'll find that the customization allowed by DNA-coding will greatly increase how well you can wield this machine. Voice commands will fill the gap that the movement slave system leaves."

Zuzu saw the system monitor come up in her visor. "All systems are green. I'm off."

"Good hunting, Vice Admiral." Azazel said, and he initiated the launch sequence. Red Eyes held firm as the walkway retracted. The red eyes on the bull head lit up, and the clamps holding the arms and legs in place released. The warship-sized robot flexed its arms and let loose a great roar.

"For the glory of Babylon!" Zuzu said, and *Minotaur* blinked out of the hangar bay. She appeared next to *Revenge*, off to her starboard side. She took an asteroid in each hand, locked on to the nearest enemy ships, and launched those rocks at them. Too close to avoid them, the destroyers from the New Prussia Reserve Fleet tried to shoot them down with concentrated point-defense and main battery fire, but to no avail. The impacts crushed both ships, destroying and sinking them in moments.

"Zuzu!" Gori said, still on *Revenge*'s bridge. "I've retrieved the captain. We can stay with the carriers if you can go on the offense."

"Feel the Fires of Baal!" Zuzu bellowed, and she fired the massive heat ray from *Minotaur*'s mouth, the one that destroyed Prince Charles. She swept the beam across the rest of the that New Prussia squadron, slicing through those frigates and destroyers with ease, sinking them all and wiping them out.

Back inside Hell's Heart, Azazel monitored *Minotaur*'s, Zuzu's, performance.

"Does *Minotaur* meet your expectations?" Red Eyes said as he approached Azazel.

"Everything installed is working as intended." The fallen angel shifted some virtual windows around. "The fleet is nearly ready to depart."

"Good. With Zuzu out there, the rest of our fleet will be able to withdraw."

On *Revenge*'s bridge, Dashing Jack arrived. "Captain on the bridge!" Gori said, dusting off the chair. Jack saluted, smiled, and took his seat.

"Status, Gori."

"Zuzu's more than able to handle them now, and with that display she's forcing them to focus their attention upon her." Gori brought up the current battle map on the main screen. "They've lost two squadrons before we played the trump card, and the fortress's guns have done well at keeping the rest at bay."

"You know the High Admiral won't let them withdraw with the girl." Jack said with a sigh, "He could easily accept a mutual withdrawal, and recapture the Countess another time, but I get the feeling that Lord Roland struck at his pride."

"What makes you say that?"

"Roland's departure out of Hell's Heart makes me say that." Jack said, "There's no way he didn't get in that mecha without making a show of it, and if he fought the High Admiral man-to-man then he had to have come away with a scarring blow. Watch how this develops, Gori. Zuzu will go on the offensive, with the aim of locating and stealing back the girl, when it's enough to cover our retreat until Hell's Heart itself is ready to go."

"Speaking of which, the Vice Admiral's actions have had the intended effect already. They're letting the carriers go in favor of dealing with

Minotaur."

"Then don't wait for the High Admiral to give the order. Recall the Goblins and the Hobgoblins. Their role in this battle is over."

As the recall order went out, Zuzu resumed weaponizing asteroids into dirt-cheap kinetic-kill vehicles. The allied fleet reorganized itself yet again, focusing its arms at Minotaur now, seeing it as more important to handle. The fleet's combined naval bombardment converged upon the massive robot, but Zuzu didn't seem to care. Thrown asteroids soon smashed the smaller ships, shattering and sinking them.

The losses mounted, and aboard *MacBeth* Ireton's mood shifted to match the tactical turn.

"How could I have not seen this coming?"

"The fleet's requesting withdrawal." The Communications Officer said.

"Granted. Fall back to New Edinburgh." Ireton said, "Get out of here before that monster kills us all."

Zuzu noticed. "Too late, fools! Now you burn!"

* * *

Back inside Hell's Heart, Red Eyes and Azazel look on. Red Eyes is amused. "Exactly as I had hoped."

"And how shall you determine which ship has the prize?"

Red Eyes paused for a moment before getting on the comms. "Zuzu, find Ireton's flagship. She's there. Cripple it. Jack, as soon as she's done that come in and board her."

"Jack, Gori, you're in a better position." Zuzu said, "Find the flagship. I'm busy smashing smaller ships."

Jack and Gori relayed the order, and their Communications Officer went to work on it while Ramsey rallied the remaining allied mecha behind him. He maneuvered around *Minotaur*'s rear, just above the neckline, and the other mecha trailed him.

"Fire what you've got at all the usual suspects: eyes, ears, joints, seams, whatever looks like it'll crack under concentrated fire", Ramsey said as he opened with his beam rifle. Beam fire, rocket volleys, missiles, and more all hit *Minotaur* in all the places Ramsey pointed out. The remaining ships, pulling back and spreading out, did the same with their guns and missiles. The guns hit all over and so did the missiles, but all that ordinance left little more than scratches.

"Is that all you've got?" Zuzu said, cackling.

"Swarm the beast!" Ramsey said, "Get in as close as you can and fire right into those points. Make her waste time on you."

114

With Ramsey leading the way, they did just that. Forced to deal with the threat of one or more of them prying open something to shoot straight into the internal structure, Zuzu tried to swat at them as if they were flies or gnats.

"Withdraw!" Ireton yelled, "All ships, withdraw!"

The smaller ships, being far closer, immediately turned about and threw open their engines to burn away at full thrust. The carriers also turned about despite being in the rear with the battleships and heavier cruisers, ready to withdraw once they retrieved their mecha. The battleships and cruisers kept up the barrage, covering the big withdrawal, but Zuzu was having none of it.

"Enough!" Zuzu said, "All of you shall burn! Baal's Fire shall consume you all!"

"Get back!" Ramsay said, "We've done enough. Get to the carriers and get out of here!"

The other mecha dispersed, spreading out in all directions before turning about and heading for the rear, which saved some of their lives when Zuzu unleashed a massive beam towards the fleet. Some of the pilots were too close, got caught, and went down. The same beam also caught several escaping smaller ships, one of the carriers, and the battleship *McClintock* from the Lone Star Kingdom.

"This is the Lord Admiral." Ireton said, "The remaining mecha, carriers, and escorts have withdrawn to the rear."

"Go!" Ramsey said, "Sibley, bring the ship in. We'll hold this beast off together."

* * *

Redalen's Revenge watched as the last of the carriers reached the jump point, took on the last of the surviving Goblins, and then jumped away.

"That leaves us, Zuzu in *Minotaur*, and the High Admiral in Hell's Heart", Gori said. "Captain, what should we do now?"

"We should prepare to retreat." Jack said, "But we have support orders. Helm move us into support position to assist *Minotaur*. Navigation, plot an escape course."

"We should go, but you're ordering that we stay."

"I said to move us into position. I didn't say at best speed. Steady as she goes, Helm."

First the Helmsman and then the Navigation Officer answer, "Aye-aye, Captain!"

"And the boarding party?" Gori said.

"Oh, I'll go lead that if it comes to it. The High Admiral won't have much room to criticize me if I'm facing the fire", Jack said. "Besides, with the losses we've taken he can't afford to cut us off. We've got the biggest guns in the fleet, and the best pilots. If he wasn't so obsessed with his grand ego totems, he'd be here, and this would be his flagship."

"Ah, yes. 'Hell's Heart is indestructible!' and all that."

"Weapons", Jack said, "as soon as you can get a lock on their flagship, isolate their engines."

"Aye-aye, Captain!"

"Let's hope that the High Admiral, at the least, is where you think he is, Captain." Gori said, "Or we're in far worse trouble than we are now."

Back in Hell's Heart, with nothing else of use to do, Red Eyes returned to Azazel's workshop. As he entered, the angel didn't bother to greet him and instead kept his eyes on the many viewscreens displaying data or other information.

"High Admiral, the jump engines are ready. We can go on your command. I presume you shall recall *Minotaur*?"

"No." Red Eyes said, "She's on a tear, and about to cripple Ireton's flagship. Then Jack will come in to board the ship and seize the prize."

Azazel looked over to the battlemap and saw that these movements were indeed happening, and that *Revenge* wasn't moving at the speed one expects. "You do realize that we can get at the girl at any time, High Admiral. You risk vital assets without need to attempt it at this time."

"Oh? Are you now making this your problem?"

"Merely giving advice, as I agreed to previously. Though, given that I've seen men wage war for ages on end, I would like you to consider that I understand what is going on better than you do, and therefore that I comprehend that persisting at this stage is needless."

"It will be worth the risk if we succeed and given what I'm seeing it seems the odds are in our favor. The demoralization effect alone will be worth the risk."

"No", Azazel said, stopping what he'd been doing and facing the warlord eye-to-eye. "They will deem us a serious threat. You know that our enemies possess their own counterparts to *Minotaur*, many of which are superior to it. You forget that it, like *Anakim*, are nothing more than testbed frames for the real machines I've been working on. *Anakim* is now lost, and I have no reason to believe that *Minotaur* won't somehow follow. You've let your pride master you, High Admiral, and while I do not care if you or the others survive this battle, neither am I so cavalier with my own existence to follow such folly."

An alert sounded. "Jump sequence initiated. T-60 minutes and counting."

"*Minotaur* can get back here in that time." Azazel said, staring at Red Eyes. "The jump cannot be stopped. Let's see which happens first: you see sense and order the Vice Admiral's withdrawal, she succeeds and withdraws with the prize, or she's compelled to withdraw by the enemy."

Red Eyes felt an anger swell up in him, but Azazel was not his subordinate. It reminded him of his father's rebukes when he was a child:

powerless to resist, and unable to retort.

"Oh, and that knight? He's right about you. You are too vain for your own good."

Red Eyes got on the comms. "Zuzu, status."

"I've located the enemy flagship, High Admiral. I'm engaging the battleship and will soon have it arrested."

"*Revenge*, status."

"We're in position to assist. Boarding party is armed and ready to launch as soon as the Vice Admiral clears the way", Jack said.

Red Eyes gave Azazel a look of self-satisfaction, and Azazel stood there, arms folded under his chest. "T-59 minutes to jump."

"You have fifty-eight minutes. Make them count." Red Eyes said, "That is all."

On *Revenge*, Jack and Gori looked over at each other and sighed.

"Boarding party to the staging area." Jack said, "Have the jump engine ready to go as soon as the party and I return. Gori don't worry about the Vice Admiral. I want you to keep a way out clear; as soon as we're back aboard, we are out of here and I don't want anything getting in our way."

"Aye, Captain. Breeching method?"

"If Zuzu does her job, that ship will be at rest and unable to resist until we breech. We're going in as close to the target as we can."

"Where will she be?"

"In the duke's quarters, so in or near the Captain's quarters" Jack said, bringing up an image of *MacBeth* and pointing to a spot amidships. "Which puts us, I think, here."

Jack got up out of his chair and made for the elevator, descending a lower deck where the party met him. "We're pressed for time. Shaped plasma charges on the hull, then extreme violence of action. Have a rebreather handy for the girl if we need it. They also need her alive, so we need not worry about being spaced. As soon as we get the go-ahead, we move."

"Aye, Captain!"

* * *

Zuzu cackled loudly as she closed like a comet upon *MacBeth*. "Let's see you escape now!"

"Fire!" Captain Denten said, "Everything! Fire!"

MacBeth launched all her remaining missiles while firing her cannons relentlessly as *Minotaur* approached. Missiles hit, cannons hit, but *Minotaur* kept coming as if nothing happened. Zuzu glanced over her options, and she saw a weapon system she had not noticed before.

"This will do nicely!" *Minotaur* thrust forth its arms. "Fiery Fists of Baal!"

Minotaur's hands quickly came to glow red, as if they came out of a forge, and then launched like rockets out towards *MacBeth*. The red-hot hands went from fists to open hands, as if to make knife chops, as they approached the battleship. Zuzu directed them with where she looked. One sheared off the turrets, the other the point-defense guns, and then they met in the double-chop of the aft thrusters. That stroke cut through as if it were a colossal beam sword, slicing clean through, and then the hands pushed the severed thrusters away from the hull.

"Zuzu to *Revenge*. Their flagship is ready!"

Revenge appeared off to *MacBeth's* starboard bow. Anchors fired from ports on the bow, lodging into *MacBeth's* hull.

"Boarders, go!" Gori said as the ship pulled up parallel to *MacBeth* where they could easily breach and access the Captain's quarters. Revenge extended a docking ring that clamped onto *MacBeth's* hull. Jack and his marines hurried down the hallway as it extended, and they set breaching charges as soon as the clamp sealed tight. The explosion blew inward, and Jack took the lead with his beam sword ignited.

Gabriela's hands trembled, sitting in the Captain's quarters as the men outside once more fought and died for her. She reached underneath her dress and pulled out her necklace. "It's all I can do now", she said. She knelt beside the bed, taking her necklace between her hands, closed her eyes and began praying. She prayed for the men putting their lives up for her. She prayed for those who already died for her. She prayed for her noble lord coming to rescue her, and she prayed that what now seemed to be a villainous victory to be undone.

"We're closing fast", Jack said, "I have her signal."

"Here comes Roland!" Gori said, "Him and his man."

"Oh ho!" Zuzu said, and the glowing hands moved again. As Sibley took *Baden-Powell's* cannons and fired upon the anchor chains as well as the docking gangway, Ramsey took *Durendal's* beam rifle and attempted to circle about *Minotaur* to strafe the beast, only to find two red-hot hands as big as *Durendal* coming at him and forcing him to divert off that course.

"Dodge those!" Zuzu said as Ramsey began dealing with *Minotaur's* hands as if they were hostile mecha, but he found the beam rifle ineffective against them. Zuzu then locked on to *Durendal* and began powering up the heat ray while *Revenge* opened upon *Baden-Powell* with its point-defense guns while bringing its main guns to bear. Sibley saw the hostile fire get thick fast and threw *Baden-Powell* into a defensive stance dodging and weaving as much as Ramsey had to do with *Durendal*, a development that Duke Ireton and Captain Denten on the bridge of *MacBeth* didn't notice.

"Jerry," Ireton said, "I didn't think it could turn around this badly this fast."

"My Lord Admiral, the fleet's coming back around."

"Do they want to die?"

Minotaur's hands completely consumed Ramsey's attention. "I'm in trouble here."

"My lord, I'm not able to assist." Sibley said while firing upon *Revenge*.

Zuzu let wide her toothy smile. "Got you! Burn in the Fires of Baal!"

The heat ray erupted from *Minotaur*'s mouth. Ramsey dodged one hand, then the other, but the ray clipped *Durendal* and sliced off its legs. Stunned, the hands now moved in and tore off its arms as if tearing them from a paper doll. "I've got to punch out!" Ramsey said, and *Durendal* discorporated leaving Ramsey floating in space, seeing that the baton was now recharging.

"Ignore him!" Gori said to Zuzu. "Help me with the ship."

Ramsey saw Creton coming and held out a hand. "That's my lad!" he said, grabbing the line, "Hurry, back to the ship!"

"What's keeping you, Jack?" Zuzu said, "We're running out of time!"

Jack faced a young officer with a beam sword at the ready in one hand, and a beam shield in the other displaying House Ireton's arms, with the difference mark of the heir.

"No more, pirate. I, Count Samuel Ireton, will break you here."

"Then we're at her door", Jack said, waving his men forward. "Send the Count to his eternal reward."

The men leveled their carbines and fired.

12 *OKLAHOMA* ARRIVES

"Captain", *Revenge*'s Navigation Officer said, "I have five vessels coming out of hyperspace from 12 o'clock, well above the plane, and on an attack vector."

"What?" Gori said as the five ships emerged. One battleship, four cruisers.

Aboard *MacBeth*, Ireton and Captain Denten saw the same thing happen. "Lord Admiral! It's the *Oklahoma*! The Solar Guard has arrived!"

On the bridge of the VGSS *Oklahoma*, a tall barrel-chested man that looked more a brawler than a sailor stood up from his chair. "Fire the Main Gun. Let's lance ourselves a bull!"

Zuzu, in *Minotaur*, looked up and zoomed in on *Oklahoma*. She saw the aperture on its bow open, power coalescing, and in a moment she remembered the signature feature of the Solar Guard's *Super Cosmo*-class battleships: a spinal-mounted main gun capable, at full charge, of making a space fortress disintegrate in one shot.

"M-cannon at 25%!" *Oklahoma*'s Weapons Officer said.

"That's enough", the Captain said, and then he ordered as if punching Minotaur himself: "Fire!"

A brilliant golden lance of a beam erupted from the bow of *Oklahoma*. Zuzu reflexively threw up *Minotaur*'s arms while trying to get out of the way. The beam pierced both arms at the forearm while she held them overhead, and then sheared off the face at the nose joint, burned into the chestplate, and scored the right leg before blowing off half the right foot.

"Pull back, Zuzu!" Gori said, "That battleship's gun can incinerate you!"

Ireton saw *Oklahoma*'s captain appear on his viewscreen. "You made it!"

"My apologies, Lord Admiral." Holm said with a laugh as he saluted, "Captain Sir Kenneth Holm and *Oklahoma*, reporting for duty. We were delayed, and it could not be avoided. By your leave, we'll finish rescuing you."

"Granted!"

Holm cut his comms. "*Arrowhead*, take the other cruisers and relieve *MacBeth*. Force that battleship to run. We'll stay on the super robot."

The four *Arrowhead*-class cruisers, featuring the first of its class, broke off from *Oklahoma* and squared up against *Redalen's Revenge*. Gori, seeing the obvious, called to Jack. *Oklahoma*'s primary turrets now powered up and opened fire upon *Minotaur* while coming around her flank at combat speed.

"Forget the girl!" Gori said. "We have four Solar Guard cruisers on approach, and they're fresh. Abort, Captain! ABORT!"

Jack heard over *MacBeth*'s internal comms that those ships and *Oklahoma* had arrived, and that *Oklahoma* had bloodied *Minotaur*. He looked at Count Samuel Ireton, his beam shield now overloaded, and saluted him. "Your deliverance has arrived, my lord. I shall have to test you another time."

Samuel held his stance as he watched Jack and the pirate boarders back away in withdrawal. He got on the comms. "Let them go. They must run now, so let them. We've done our job. Guide them out and seal the section they breached."

Jack lead his men back the way they came, running now as fast as they could. The bulkheads closed behind them one by one, until they got back to where they breached and ran back across the docking gangway. Once the Iretons sealed that section off, the clamps disengaged, and the gangway retracted. Jack got across first, and then he turned back to see his men follow. It was after half made it that the first volley of cruiser fire struck, severing both anchor chains as well as the retracting gangway. Several of his men got vaporized in the blast, with no others surviving. With a clenched fist, he turned inside and got back through the airlock.

"Gori, get us out of here!"

On *Oklahoma*'s bridge, Captain Holm threw open a deep laugh as *Revenge* engaged her thrusters and broke away from *MacBeth*. "Oh? You think you're getting away now?"

"Missiles incoming!" *Revenge*'s Weapons Officer said as more primary beam cannon fire from the *Arrowhead*s slammed against *Revenge*'s shields. Her point-defense cannons threw up plenty enough fire to shoot them down, but Gori could see the fatigue setting in on the bridge. Jack saw it as he made his way back to the bridge.

"Captain on the bridge!" Gori said.

"As you were. We have no time for formalities, not if we want to stay alive", Jack took his seat. "Are we ready to jump?"

Jack opened a channel. "Vice Admiral, *Revenge* must withdraw. Good luck."

Zuzu, her body wracked with pain, tried to keep her bearings as *Oklahoma* pounded *Minotaur* with her primary cannons.

"Damn you Jack!" Zuzu screamed.

"We have four fresh cruisers on our tail, Zuzu. We're in no position to help you. Pull back to Hell's Heart."

Zuzu's rage took over, and that became manifest in *Minotaur*. The inexplicable bull's roar bellowed forth once more, and now Zuzu only had eyes for the dart-like battleship menacing her with its primary cannons.

"We've got the bull's full attention now", Captain Holm said. "Let's get her away from *MacBeth*. *Baden-Powell*, respond."

Ramsey came on his screen. "I can't hold that many aboard, Captain, but I can get the Lord Admiral and the Countess away. You'll have to return later for the rest of the crew."

"I'll leave that to you then, my lord", Holm said. "Get them and get out."

"Understood." Ramsey said, and he cut off. As *Oklahoma* played the matador to *Minotaur*, Sibley brought *Baden-Powell* alongside *MacBeth* and extended a hatch. Once clamped and attached, Ramsey went down to retrieve Duke Ireton and Gabriela. He found them on the bridge, along with Count Samson. Gabriela, upset, threw her arms around Ramsey. As he held her in his arms, Ramsey looked up at Ireton.

"Your Grace," Ramsey said, "it's time for the Lord Admiral to transfer his flag."

Ireton nodded and turned to Captain Denten. "Don't die, Jerry."

Denten saluted. "Come on, son" Ireton turned to leave." Time to go."

"You too, my lady." Ireton said, and she held to Ramsey as they left *MacBeth* to board *Baden-Powell*.

* * *

"I told you that this was not a wise course of action." Azazel said, not even looking up from his monitors.

"T-42 minutes and counting." The automated announcement said, "Jump imminent."

"She's just got to get past the pain and then she'll see that she can just run Roland's ship down, slice it open, and take the girl. She can do that and get back here in time." Red Eyes glanced over at the monitor, which displayed the schematics for a robot dubbed "Gilgamesh".

"You would sacrifice your sister to secure a prize that can be more easily captured another time? High Admiral, your priorities are askew."

"It's not like you care. You've already moved on from Minotaur, haven't you?"

"The Solar Guard's *Super Cosmo*-class of battleships is capable of destroying *Minotaur*, and I am confident that this ship's captain is smart enough to realize that. He's not playing dumb, High Admiral. He's figured out that Zuzu's using a force-feedback system to control *Minotaur*, so he's using that to his advantage to keep Zuzu fixated on that ship while the others get away."

"And Jack's got to let her go." Red Eyes said with an exasperated huff.

"Yes, and you're going to let him withdraw because you know that you need him and his ship." Azazel shifted over to a schematic to a smaller mecha design, dubbed "Endiku". "Your problem is that you don't like to not win decisively. Nevermind losing, you get angered when you don't win like you want. It's a stupid way to think, and it will destroy you if you don't rip it out of your mind like the cancer it is. This time you have the excuse of Jack being pursued by four *Arrowhead*-class cruisers coordinating against Jack's *Revenge*, so it doesn't hurt so much to let him flee, but you can't do that with *Minotaur* now can you?"

"*Revenge* to Hell's Heart. We're leaving." Jack said, "See you at the rendezvous point."

A moment later, *Redalen's Revenge* disappeared from Hell's Heart's sensors. "Yes, we shall." Red Eyes said. His mind raced now trying to figure out how to make this go the way he wants.

"T-minus 41 minutes. Jump imminent."

"Now Ireton can take one of those cruisers for his flagship."

"Unlikely." Azazel swiped to another schematic, marked "Hobgoblin Mk.2". "The duke is stubborn about his family pride, so he'll make Roland transfer him to one of his own ships, inadequate as they may be, instead of being expedient and using a Guard ship until he can get away and regroup."

"You're certain of this?"

"Yes." Azazel input the Mk. 2 schematics into the control systems. "His choice of flagship, division of the fleet, and how he ran the battle demonstrated a sensitivity to his family's status that could have been exploited to your benefit, but it's too late now."

"Why didn't you say this before the battle?"

"You didn't ask." Azazel brought back the "Enkidu" schematics, input them, and then queued up build orders for both designs out of the Manufacturing Wing. "That's yet another flaw of yours, High Admiral, and it has cost you severely. You presume too much, and pay too little attention to details, one of which being the conditions of my collaboration with you. So caught up in fulfilling my price that you lost sight of why you're paying it. No wonder Jack routinely beats you at both Chess and Go."

"At least I can win against him in other amusements."

"None that transform men into rulers, or commanders, of merit. So caught up in your savage ways that you forget why civilized militaries routinely destroy savage mobs, because charismatic leadership and personal valor only go so far once you are at the size you wish to operate. The result of your lacking is that when someone of superior acumen comes along, they make your prowess work against you and turn your charisma into a farce."

Red Eyes turned his attention back to Zuzu. "Break off from that battleship. Seize Roland's ship and hit the recall button. Hurry!"

Zuzu broke off and away from *Oklahoma*. As she returned to where *MacBeth* lay helpless, as it was the last time she saw it, she scanned for *Baden-Powell* and found it on the edge of Minotaur's sensors, mixed up with the rest of Ireton's fleet. *Oklahoma* followed hot on her heels, firing away, and *MacBeth*'s lifeboats streamed away as fast as they could go, which proved wise when Zuzu smashed the battleship until it exploded when she hit the magazine.

"Where are you?" she bellowed, and then it came up clear again on her sensors. She locked it in and shot off in pursuit, clearing space in seconds, and causing a panic in Ireton's ranks. Now aboard a cruiser, *MacLeod*, Ireton ordered a retreat. Ships in the rear of the formation turned about and, having spun up their hyperdrives, jumped away immediately. Others soon followed, and with each ship's escape Zuzu grew angrier as the odds of her getting all of the targets she desired slipped further away.

But *Baden-Powell* remained, intent on covering the retreat before doing so themselves, and that Zuzu determined to be enough. *MacLeod* now turned about and began to spin up her drives as her thrusters took her away from the oncoming beast machine. *Baden-Powell* fired upon it, aiming for damaged parts such as the shorn face, putting Zuzu into pain as it struck *Minotaur*'s internal structure, but just as *MacLeod* cleared enough distance and time to jump away *Minotaur* closed on *Baden-Powell* and attempted to seize it with both hands.

Zuzu forgot about *Oklahoma*. The battleship fired a full volley from its primary cannons upon Minotaur, striking it square in the back, and the shock of the hits filled Zuzu with pain. That pain kept Zuzu from seizing *Baden-Powell*, which moved to rendezvous with *Oklahoma*.

"The prize is gone. Returning to base." Zuzu said.

* * *

Duke Ireton, on the bridge of *MacLeod*, sat deep into the captain's chair. His son, Samuel, held Gabriela as she struggled to keep it together.

"*Oklahoma*", Ireton said, "we can do no more good here. Withdraw to New Edinburgh."

"Understood, Lord Admiral. We'll take up the rearguard, just in case, while the rest of the fleet withdraws."

"Don't despair for Lord Roland." Samson said softly to Gabriela, "He will prevail and return to us."

MacLeod turned about on a heading for New Edinburgh. The other ships jumped ahead of her, and then *MacLeod*'s captain gave the order and she too was away. *Oklahoma* observed their departure, and as she did the captains of her cruiser escorts appeared on screen with Captain Holm.

"We're not leaving just yet." Holm said, "Project the trajectory of *Revenge*'s departure and get me likely points of exit along that line. Go retrieve anyone still alive. I've got a private transmission to make."

Holm left the bridge for his quarters. When he got there, he pulled up his terminal and called back up to the bridge to get connected back to Earth on a priority channel. A moment later an old man with the crest of Archangel Michael on his breast appeared.

"Captain", Duke Michael said, "I'd been expecting Lord Roland."

"He's trailing the beast."

124

Holm brought up combat footage taken of *Minotaur*, especially how it destroyed *Durendal*, and showed it to the old duke.

"That's a Super Robot, Captain."

"From what I heard, that one robot is the one responsible for the prior fleet's destruction, and it inflicted a lot of damage in this action before we arrived. None of their mecha, not even *Durendal*, did more than minor damage to it. Until we hit her with *Oklahoma*'s M-cannon, she was invincible."

"What's Duke Ireton's status?"

"The reprisal action met its objective, but several participating squadrons got wiped out or severely damaged. A second dispatch isn't viable, Your Grace. The best that can happen is that my squadron goes on alone, and for all we can do that isn't enough against the enemy's fleet. We'll be swarmed and destroyed for certain. These are preventable losses, Your Grace, but only you are your peers are in a position to make it so."

"I see", the old duke drummed his fingers. "I will move on this now, as time is not our friend today. Go with God, Captain."

"Likewise, Your Grace." Holm said, saluting.

Captain Holm disappeared from Duke Michael's screen. He hit a button and two other old men appeared.

"Raphael, Gabriel, it is as we suspected. They have the capacity to manufacture and deploy Super Robots. Lord Roland needs that power."

"You want to authorize *Roland*'s deployment?" Gabriel said.

"I do."

"Michael, if it weren't for your fastidiousness, some might say that this is softness for your protege", Raphael said. "I give authorization."

"Likewise."

"Then you all know what to do."

Each man opened a window on their screen where they got prompted to enter their authentication codes, and then place their bare hand on a scanner. One by one each man's authentication came back green and the screen progressed to a list of nine Solar Guard Super Robots. They each selected *Roland*, and a prompt came up asking to confirm authorization, which they each gave.

"It's done." Michael said. "Now it's up to Roland."

"On the larger matter", Gabriel said, "what do we know now?"

"They've rescued Countess Gabriela, but the cost was far higher than expected", Michael said. "Most of the pirate fleet escaped, including their fortress. This is just the beginning, my friends. While our battleships can deal with this one pirate Super Robot, I don't think we'll be able to count on that for much longer."

"Then we know that the fallen one is there for certain?" Raphael said.

"We do, and once Lord Roland returns, I will debrief him and get more information on this matter", Michael said. "I want you two listening privately when I do so."

"Understood." they said.

"No matter how much of a charismatic warlord this pirate Red Eyes is, or how ambitious he is, the manufacturing of a fleet and fielding of a private navy is not within one such man's grasp."

"He has to have allies", Gabriel said. "There is no other way to get that many men under his banner without anyone noticing."

"We've suspected treason within Christendom for some time. This just makes the argument more substantial, but it's persuasive only to those already friendly to it", Raphael said. "Our friends in the Court of Stars report that many find this pirate episode only of peripheral concern, even with the Countess's abduction."

"Count Qis' speech was quite persuasive", Gabriel said.

"Yes, it was, and very timely. So was the attempted poisoning after that." Michael said.

"I would like to believe that he is not in league with them", Gabriel said.

"We'll see soon enough", Raphael said. "If something somehow afflicts the Countess despite all the valor displayed for her benefit, killing or incapacitating her, then we can turn our eyes his way. She is the only one left to give an account of things, and if hers doesn't come in accord with the rest then we know something larger is wrong with this."

* * *

Count Qis walked into his office in the family's residence on Earth outside of Oslo, Norway. "Secure the premises. I will have no eavesdropping."

The servant bowed and left the room, passing the order along. A few minutes later, after another servant delivered Qis his coffee, he got a notification that his will had been done. He drew the curtains and donned the hood that concealed his face before answering a call on his desk's viewscreen. When he did, Red Eyes appeared as a hologram before him.

"Master," Red Eyes said, kneeling before Qis, "Duke Ireton's reprisal lead to an unfortunate complication."

"Yes", Qis said, his void cold as the north wind of a Norwegian winter. "I am aware of your failure to fulfill your end of your bargain with the angel."

"But I have *Minotaur*, and I can easily-"

Qis's face, such as could be seen, turned to a scowl. "Why did you waste precious time on such an irrelevance?!"

Red Eyes's face revealed first his surprise as Qis' rebuke and then a flash of anger at the blow to his pride. "But Master, I-"

"FOOL! You risked everything, forgot your objective, for a useless display of glory? Have you considered the consequences?"

"But-"

"HAVE YOU?"

Red Eyes stood there, stunned into silence.

"What possible consequence could come of Roland's presence? Did you consider that? Do you think that you're the only one able to deploy a Super Robot?"

"But there's no-"

"Your own robot can be jumped across hyperspace to where the pilot requires it. You've got as an enemy someone able to conjure a mech from a baton. Did you forget who the pilots of the Solar Guard's Super Robots are?"

Now Azazel stepped into frame. "He did."

"What would you have me do?"

Qis's face, such as Red Eyes could see it, turned from dismay to disgust. "Withdraw."

Red Eyes' face showed the shock at his master's disdain for his need for glory.

"You are to do nothing but recover your losses and prepare for the next operation. Am I understood?"

Red Eyes sighed. "Yes, Master. Victory for Babylon!"

"Victory for Babylon!" Qis said, and he nodded to Azazel before he cut off his connection.

* * *

Duchess Ireton found Countess Gabriela Robin knelt in prayer, hands clasped about her necklace, in the Chapel of Scarborough Castle. The duchess approached Gabriela quietly, not announcing her presence, and knelt beside her. It was another moment or so before Gabriela looked up and noticed her there.

"I've only been here a moment, my dear", Ireton said. "Our confessor asked me to speak with you. His Excellency the Grand Bishop worries about you, as does my husband and son."

Gabriela smiled as she wiped a tear from her face. "It is one thing to read tales of romance, to thrill at the idea of a man's display of valor on behalf of a lady, but to see it with one's own eyes."

"You see with the eyes of a loving heart, my dear."

"All these men. They have mothers. They have daughters. They have wives, or they are betrothed, or otherwise loved. They did what those tales bade of them, and so many of them will not come home. They died, slain in an instant if merciful, or screaming if not, as they look upon their last moments in horror."

Ireton took Gabriela's hands into her own. "Including two of my sons."

"And yet you are not cross with me?"

127

Ireton now embraced the Countess. "Because they died for God and their Duke, my dear, doing the duties demanded of them. They died with honor, and while I would rather have them alive, I cannot be cross with a death suffered for the good our people or for Christendom. No mother worth her virtue would ever be so cross, and in you is not just a beautiful woman, but the hope of all Christendom symbolized in your presence. It was not just for you that they fought and died, my dear, but all that is bound up within you. The songbird is God's earthly reflection of the heavenly choir, which is why it is an honor to be called a songbird, as one who sings as you do sings like the angels themselves."

Gabriela felt a weight shift about her heart. "Then let their deaths not be in vain."

"Pray for the living as well as the dead", Ireton said. "My husband tells me that Lord Roland's comrades have already rescued a few score left adrift in space after their ships or mecha got destroyed, and then there is the hero yet engaged with the enemy."

"Roland."

"Yes. He needs our prayers most urgently."

Gabriela now remembered the transmitter she concealed. "Wait. We can do more than pray. We can be heard right in the heart of the enemy, or at least wherever Roland's ship is, with this."

"A faint hope, but a hope nonetheless."

"Your Grace, I have an idea. Call to the families in mourning. Ask for the women loved by the honorable dead to come. We shall come together and give song in prayer for those yet in the fight, that God may deliver them from that hell."

Duchess Ireton thought on the idea. "A chorus, you say?"

"Yes, a chorus of the widowed and the orphaned, that Heaven hears our cries and sees fit to bring justice to the villains who brought untimely death to our people."

"Here, at the Chapel?"

"Yes, here."

"I know whom to call, and I shall make the arrangements. My husband, my son, and His Excellency the Grand Bishop will be relieved to see you standing forth once more."

Ireton saw a playful smile come forth on Gabriela's face.

"You say that the Guard's ships are still in the area?"

"Yes."

"Maybe they would like to participate? They would have to know how to raise Lord Roland's ship, would they not? If we can transmit our song to them, and they repeat it on whatever channels they have to get a hold of his ship-"

"Of course, my dear. I will make the request. I doubt he will deny you."

Then the two turned back to finish their prayers. They prayed for the dead. They prayed for the missing. They prayed for those left lame, those widowed, those orphaned, those who were the last of their line, and many more, before they turned their prayers to Ramsey. There they focused on beseeching Saint Itano the Gunner, Saint Fokker the Pilot, Saint Musashi the Swordsman, the Archangel Michael, and many others to bring their words before God in the name of His Son Jesus Christ that He might aid Ramsey in overcoming Red Eyes and escaping from the warlord, that He might deliver Ramsey from Hell's Heart.

Word of the initiative spread before Her Grace the Duchess called upon the widows and mothers of men she knew had died in combat. The Grand Bishop called up the Archbishops of New Edinburgh and asked them to hold a special Mass in this vein, and they--excited by the idea--informed their dioceses to do so. Guardsmen in the castle talked about it to their families, and their wives and mothers and sisters talked about it as they went about their daily work. Soon all New Edinburgh knew of the countess's proposal and they gathered at their parishes. Gabriela had her wish within 30 minutes.

"Of course," Duke Ireton said. "I shall contact *Oklahoma* and let you petition the captain directly."

Captain Sir Kenneth Holm heard the Duchess's petition, and he laughed. "Fantastic idea! By His Grace's leave, we'll move to where Lord Roland is hold there for your transmission. Once he comes forth from that fortress, we'll be certain to get their attention so he's clear to escape. Tell our lady the countess that we shall be ready to deliver her song of love when she's ready."

13 DELIVER ME FROM HELL

Baden-Powell rested alongside Oklahoma.

"Red Eyes' pride is hurt", Ramsey said to Captain Holm. "If we press him, then he'll make *Minotaur* come out for us again."

"I think I know where you're going with this", Holm said.

"Sit at maximum range, target that fortress, and begin charging the M-cannon. Take your time, Captain. We need the dread more than the execution."

"That will certain force their super robot out", Holm said. "Now to prove that I'm on your wavelength. Check your armor, my lord."

Ramsey looked to see that he now had access to his super robot, and he smiled. "You talked to the old man, didn't you?"

"It gets better", Sibley said." The Countess organized a live performance to begin shortly, and she aimed to aid you with music."

Ramsey smiled. "I see."

"I'll be ready to transmit when ready", Sibley said.

"We've got Red Eyes in a no-win situation", Ramsey said. "Either he saves his fortress by jumping away as soon as possible, or he saves his robot and her pilot but gets stuck here and captured."

"My lord", Holm said. "I think we know how this ends."

Red Eyes walked down the main hallway from the Grand Hall to the Docking Bay as *Minotaur* returned.

"We still have a half-hour until we jump, Sister. You're not done yet."

Zuzu could not believe her ears. "You're joking."

"No", Red Eyes said as he looked up at *Minotaur*. "We're not ready to jump just yet, and there are hostile forces able to interfere. You have to stop them."

"I am in great pain, Brother", Zuzu said. "I cannot win if they don't hold back."

Red Eyes put a hand on the damaged *Minotaur*. "You need only hold them back until the last moment. Recall at the final moment and that will be sufficient."

Red Eyes put his other hand and his head on *Minotaur*. "I am sorry, Sister. It is this, or we lose everything. We cannot allow that battleship to fire its main gun. Less than half an hour, Sister, that is all I ask of you."

Zuzu nodded, tears of pain streaming down her face. "Victory for Babylon."

Minotaur turned about and walked back out into space. Once in space, it took off towards *Oklahoma*'s location.

* * *

Azazel stood at his workshop in the Manufacturing Wing. He had the spectacle in the Docking Bay on in another window, when he picked up an unidentified signal. . It took him some time to isolate the signal, since it wasn't an analog signal transmission, but he found it when he switched to a digital signal sweep.

"Interesting."

He found the band, and then found the stream itself to be encrypted. Since the signal began at *Baden-Powell*, Azazel reasoned that this was a secured channel for the Solar Guard, and what they discussed was very time-sensitive. This eliminated any possibility of brute-force breaking of the encryption, but he could run a trace. In yet another window he brought up a traceroute map, on a galactic scope, and routed the signal back first to a nearby system and then to New Edinburgh. Then he detected a second signal hidden within the first, this one coming from Earth, but it was a burst in comparison to the primary signal.

"Ah-ha!" he said, "So that's how they do it."

He also noticed that another signal, the one he knew Dashing Jack set up previously, still had a passive receptor in Ramsey's vessel. Putting the two together gave the fallen angel a flash of self-satisfaction.

Now he looked back at the window monitoring the spectacle in the Docking Bay, and he smiled as he looked on at Red Eyes beseeching Zuzu to sortie one more time.

"Let's see if you're doing what I think you're doing, young Roland." Azazel moved the traceroute data to a nondescript folder labeled "Boredom Breakers" and then glanced at the family drama again. "The High Admiral could use a broken nose."

Red Eyes saluted Zuzu as she left. "Victory for Babylon."

Zuzu locked on to *Oklahoma*. She kept a timer on Hell's Heart's jump engines, now at T-25 minutes. "Just a little longer."

Zuzu picked up *Baden-Powell* alongside *Oklahoma*, and *Oklahoma* was charging its main gun. She then noticed Ramsey standing on the dorsal hull of *Baden-Powell*.

"What is he doing?" Zuzu said, confused.

"Have you ever heard the tale of Pope Simon I?" Ramsey said on open comms. "It is not a tale a savage like you would know."

Inside, Sibley gasped at the mention of the first post-Cataclysm pope, the warrior pope, the hero born a miner's son in the Appalachian Mountains of North America.

"What trickery is this?" Zuzu said, still closing into firing range.

"Simon was a warrior, a fighting man, and a priest in one of the armies of Old Earth before he became Pope in the wake of the Cataclysm."

Zuzu felt that this was a trick. "Enough talk!" she said, and she targeted Ramsey. "You're up to something."

* * *

Countess Gabriela smiled as the ladies and goodwives called upon gathered in the Chapel of Scarborough Castle. These were the daughters, wives, and mothers of Ireton soldiers and sailors slain in combat on her behalf. They came because they heard what she wanted to do, and with the permission and assistance of the Grand Bishop she organized them into a choir with herself as both lead soloist and conductor. Gabriela's friends Olga, Maya, and Conte aided her in getting the ladies into the mindset of a choir quickly and the idea changed into a special Mass service lead by the Grand Bishop.

"When the time comes, we shall sing", Gabriela told them. "His Grace the Duke has arranged for us to operate remotely like this, so we don't disrupt the Mass with security concerns."

The time came, and Conte monitored the service, so he could signal to Gabriela when thire time arrived. With a gesture he signaled to Gabriela that they were live. The Grand Bishop had already introduced her and the choir, so the ladies could get right to their work. Without a word, she came forth and curtsied. The ladies of the choir then did likewise. With Gabriela in the lead, standing before the choir, she faced the camera and began to sing.

The signal flashed across the stars, where Captain Holm of *Oklahoma* repeated to *Baden-Powell*. Sibley saw it come up, and he immediately threw it up on open comms so Zuzu and Red Eyes would hear it.

"Do you hear that?" Ramsey said, still standing on *Baden-Powell*'s hull. "That's an ancient lament, pirate. Even now, the lady you know only as a prize to seize and fence like everything else you steal comes forth to pray for the deliverance of your soul, a mercy that you are not worthy of receiving."

Zuzu's confusion turned to frustration. "This is your scheme? To soothe me like some animal?"

"Listen to the wisdom of Pope Simon", Ramsey said. "He said 'Do not believe in yourself, for that is not enough to overcome the foul powers of this world'."

Zuzu felt something coming up from deep within her, a primal anger and rage like that of a disobedient child being rebuked by her father, and it seized her.

Ramsey continued. "He said, 'Do not believe in others, for they are like you and that is not enough to overcome those foul powers'."

Zuzu gave himself over to the spirit of her line, and an inhuman scream came forth from her. "Enough!"

"He said 'Believe in the Lord, for through Him you shall do the impossible.'" Ramsey now looked at his bracer, seeing that his namesake unit was ready and waiting.

Zuzu targeted Ramsey, and *Minotaur*'s hands lit up.

"He said 'Through Him you shall see the invisible'." Ramsey stared out at where *Minotaur* was, unconcerned.

Zuzu watched the distance to target count down.

"He said 'Through Him you shall touch the untouchable'." Ramsey said.

Zuzu finalized her targeting. The Firey Hands of Baal were at full charge.

"He said 'Through Him you shall break the unbreakable'."

Zuzu grimaced. "I have you now."

"Know this, pirate", Ramsey said. "We of the Solar Guard take those words as our creed, especially my peers and I, and now you shall see with your own eyes what deeds we can accomplish with that creed bound to our hearts. You have to face one of the militant orders to get more fearsome foes out of the Church."

"Even crippled, I can still take both of your ships" Zuzu said. "But I shall enjoy killing you first."

"Since when did I say you faced only two ships?"

* * *

Countess Gabriela, with the choir of women with war-lost men behind her, changed the tune from the lament that she sang previously. Now she sang a joyful song, a song of glory and victory, one taken from that tale of the Martian princess of Old Earth's era. Then one of her friends, Lady Olga, joined her in a duet. This seemed a new song, but Ramsey felt something familiar.

"I want to live on", Gabriela sang. As she reached the chorus, she drew out saying "I love you."

But it was the next line that made a galaxy gasp: "I won't sleep until you know the depth of me."

Captain Holm and Sibley, staying in contact, gave each other a knowing look.

"It looks like my lord has found his lioness", Holm said.

Hearing the change in Gabriela's performance inspired Ramsey. "Allow me to introduce your real foe, pirate."

Zuzu looked on from afar as Ramsey spread his arms wide. She felt terror shoot up her spine. "Firey Fists of Baal!"

Ramsey clapped his hands together. "*Roland*, come to battle!"

On Earth, in the chamber where Ramsey and his peers met on their rare occasions, the starship-sized statue of Roland the Frank lit up. Ramsey drew apart his hands, as if he had used the baton to conjure *Durendal*, as first the outline of a man-like warship-sized figure appeared. Ramsey lifted off the hull and hovered in space, settling into the chest near the heart of a living man, as the figure solidified around him. When it finished, Zuzu beheld an android rendition of that statue. From nowhere a mighty warhorn blew, echoing all about the battlefield, and somewhere in the depths of Zuzu's soul she knew what she now beheld.

"*Roland*, the Lion of France, has arrived!" Ramsey said. "What say you now, pirate?"

"You can't win against the Fires of Baal! Burn!" Zuzu said as *Minotaur* roared, opening its mouth to fire the heat ray. Meanwhiles, its Fiery Fists closed fast on *Roland*.

"Behold!" Ramsey said. "To hand, Durendal!"

Roland's hands formed into fists, and those fists met as if one held a scabbard and the other reached to draw from it. From nowhere, a blade came forth, and that blade sliced through both Firey Fists, destroying them.

"You can't win, pirate." Ramsey said. "You won't stop *Oklahoma* from destroying your fortress. Further resistance is useless. Surrender."

Ramsey had a tracker in his display tracking *Oklahoma*'s M-cannon, and at that moment it was 50% charged.

Zuzu fired the heat ray at *Roland* but seeing that firing it fixed *Minotaur* in place Ramsey rushed *Minotaur*. Zuzu cut the beam off and tried to dodge *Roland*'s charge. She looked at the jump tracker: T-15 minutes.

Zuzu roared. "Blood and gore by mighty horn!" *Minotaur*'s horns detached and flew at *Roland*, but Ramsey cut through and destroyed them also. *Roland* closed too fast for *Minotaur*, and only a dodge roll off the line of attack at the last moment saved Zuzu.

* * *

Qis watched his cousin's performance on one monitor while maintaining contact with Azazel in another.

"Time to jump?" Qis asked.

"T-10 minutes." Azazel said.

"*Minotaur* is forfeit", Qis said. "I concur with your opinion that the High Admiral needs to get his nose broken. Do not accept her recall."

"Do you think they'll fire upon Hell's Heart?"

"Fire?" Qis said. "They will fire, but just as likely will be a deliberate miss.

The rest of the Red Eyes fleet awaits its master. Jump when ready."

"Of course. We can settle up another time." Azazel said.

"On that, I have a plan."

Ramsey chased *Minotaur* around, menacing it with his sword.

"You can't win. You have nothing but your heat ray left, and if you use it you die." Ramsey pressed his point by scoring *Minotaur*'s exterior with his sword.

Zuzu grimaced as she felt the strike. "I won't let you destroy my home."

Ramsey saw the M-cannon reach 90% charge. "That's not possible."

Zuzu looked at her jump timer: T-5 minutes.

"You leave me no choice", Zuzu said. She accelerated at full speed on a collision course with *Oklahoma*.

Ramsey followed, surpassed her, and held *Roland*'s sword high. "Then you leave me with none either. You asked for this."

Zuzu ignored *Roland*, going full speed to ram with the battleship. "Victory for Babylon!"

In one smooth motion, Roland moved into *Minotaur*'s line of attack. "Lion's Lethal Lunge!"

Roland's sword thrust forward like a spear, edge held up to cut deep, and it struck *Minotaur* head-on. The keen edge sliced through *Minotaur* right down the middle, slaying Zuzu before *Minotaur*'s destruction was complete.

"God rest your soul, woman", Ramsey said as Minotaur's ruin exploded behind him.

"Ramsey", Holm said, "we're fully charged."

"Make them remember us, Captain", Ramsey said. "Sibley, get ready to track their trajectory."

Red Eyes looked on, tears streaming down his face. "I will avenge you, Sister!"

"T-minus 1 minute to jump."

"Warning!" an automated alarm said. "Incoming fire!"

Oklahoma fired her M-cannon upon Hell's Heart, deliberately avoiding a kill shot in favor of a more limited goal: its sublight engines. The shot went through and through, obliterating them, and shaking the rest of the planetoid fortress.

Red Eyes heard the auto-alarm report the damage and slammed a fist. "Damn them! We're stuck wherever we are now."

Oklahoma, Baden-Powell, and *Roland* witnessed the crippled space fortress jump away.

"That signal beacon you left will make this much easier, my lord", Sibley said.

"Get the likely routes and stop there. We'll catch up another day", Ramsey said. He brought himself back over Baden-Powell, where he released *Roland* back to Earth and then got back inside his ship.

"Time to head back to New Edinburgh for us", Ramsey said. "Captain, it's been good to work with you and your crew again."

"Back to Earth for us, my lord. Until we see each other again, farewell", Holm said, saluting.

Ramsey and Sibley returned the salute as *Oklahoma* broke off and jumped away.

Gabriela stood out among the crowd gathered to greet *Baden-Powell's* return to New Edinburgh. No sooner did Ramsey disembark than she rushed and embraced the Star Knight.

"I knew you would do it! You're wonderful!" Gabriela said.

Ramsey's face softened into a warm smile. "You're something yourself, my lady. Your aid proved valuable."

Sibley just walked around the two and greet Duke and Duchess Ireton. "Your Grace, let's go and leave them be."

The two nobles, and their entourage, looked on and nodded in agreement. Without a word, they returned to the castle and left Ramsey embracing and embraced   by   Gabriela.

ABOUT THE AUTHOR

Bradford C. Walker is an independent science fiction author, gamer, and historian living in the Minneapolis, Minnesota area with his family.

He maintains a blog, Walker's Retreat, at bradfordcwalker.blogspot.com when he's not working on the next book in the Star Knight Saga and the curious may attempt to contact him there.